FIFTY-SEVEN HEAVEN

FIFTY-SEVEN HEAVEN

LONNIE CRUSE

FIVE STAR

An imprint of Thomson Gale, a part of The Thomson Corporation

THOMSON

GALE

Detroit • New York • San Francisco • New Haven, Conn. • Waterville, Maine • London

THOMSON

GALE

LIBRARY OF CONGRESS CATALOGING-IN-PUBLICATION DATA

Cruse, Lonnie.
  Fifty-seven heaven / Lonnie Cruse. — 1st ed.
    p. cm.
  ISBN-13: 978-1-59414-600-8 (hardcover : alk. paper)
  ISBN-10: 1-59414-600-4 (hardcover : alk. paper)
  1. Married people—Fiction. 2. Antique and classic cars—Collectors and collecting—Fiction. 3. Metropolis (Ill.)—Fiction. I. Title. II. Title: "57 heaven."
PS3603.R87F54 2007
813'.6—dc22   2000317217

First Edition. First Printing: December 2007.

Published in 2007 in conjunction with Tekno Books and Ed Gorman.

Printed in the United States of America on permanent paper
10 9 8 7 6 5 4 3 2 1

For Don Cruse, who helps me re-live
the Fabulous Fifties.
Love you most!

ACKNOWLEDGMENTS

Special thanks to the Southern Illinois Region Ohio Valley Chapter of the Antique Automobile Club of America, for their information and inspiration.

Thanks to my wonderful editor, Denise Dietz; I couldn't have done it without you!

CHAPTER ONE

"Only Will Ann Lloyd would get herself strangled with a pair of jumper cables and stuffed into the trunk of a car," my husband Jack harrumphed. "Strangled I could understand, but why did she have to pick the trunk of my classic Bel Air?"

"Honey, I seriously doubt she planned this. Even Cousin Will Ann wouldn't stoop to having herself murdered and stuffed into your trunk just to keep you from winning a trophy. She wasn't that vindictive."

His snort told me he wasn't convinced. I knew he was copping this attitude to keep from tossing his cookies. I was taking a lot of deep breaths myself. And the young police officer staring dumbfounded into the trunk of Jack's 1957 show-quality Chevy appeared to be turning that nasty shade of chartreuse so popular back in the fifties.

For years people had predicted one day someone would strangle Will Ann. I hadn't believed anyone would really carry through with it. But I wasn't about to double-check to be sure. One quick glance into the trunk had been enough for me. A fly buzzed by and I nearly gagged.

"I've called the coroner. No use calling the paramedics." The officer hitched his gun belt a notch higher, whether to intimidate us or keep his pants up was anybody's guess. Jack and I had kids older than this cop. The police department in Paducah, Kentucky must be recruiting from kindergarten these days.

Paducah was situated just a stone's throw across the river

from the small city in Southern Illinois where Jack and I had spent most of our lives. Yes, there really was a place named Metropolis, and yes, we really were known as the home of Superman. I took no responsibility for either of those facts, but I was rather fond of the huge statue of the superhero that dominated our courthouse. No southern generals dashing off to war on bronze steeds for us, thank you very much.

"The detectives are on their way, sir," the cop said to Jack. "You folks will have to stick around."

Like Jack would've left his car in someone else's hands? Me, possibly, but never his beloved Chevy. Oh, dear. That was exactly what he'd have to do. Our classic Chevy was now evidence in a murder case. They'd likely tear her apart piece by piece, just like he'd done when he restored her. Only they wouldn't put her back together with such tender loving care.

All that tedious work Jack had done, down the drain. Not to mention all the money he'd spent. eBay thrived, thanks primarily to Jack Bloodworth's frequent bids on "necessary parts." We had a small fortune carefully stored in buckets and boxes in the huge pole barn behind our home.

I turned away from my thoughts and swished over to a nearby shade tree, pink horsehair petticoat scratching my legs as my bright red poodle skirt floated above it. A too-tight ponytail was giving me a screaming headache. How had I worn my hair this way, day after day in high school, without it pulling my brains out?

Jack ran a hand through his hair, destroying the effect of the graying cootie slide he'd carefully combed over his forehead. He took another deep breath and spoke to the officer.

"I'll go tell the judges we're withdrawing my car from the competition. That will keep them from trooping through here and destroying any evidence."

The officer nodded then called after Jack when he'd barely

walked a few yards. "Just make sure you come right back here, sir. Otherwise I'll have to swear out a warrant."

"You have my wife as a guarantee I'll return," Jack called over his shoulder. "If I was going to abandon Kitty, I'd have done it several decades ago, before I married her."

I heard Jack mumble, "And before I became related to her cousin," but, thankfully, the cop didn't.

Jack yanked off his black leather jacket, tossed it over his shoulder, and marched toward the judges' tent at the center of Bob Noble Park. Honking for their daily bread, the ever-present geese flapped their way out of the large pond and quickly surrounded Jack. He sent them scurrying for cover with a frustrated wave and shout.

The young officer cocked an eyebrow at me as if deciding whether or not to slap the cuffs on. He apparently concluded that my hundred-thirty pounds weren't much of a threat to his two-hundred plus, and went back to guarding the trunk of our Chevy. The name on his tag, Officer Butwell, certainly matched his physique. I plopped down under the shade tree—choosing to avoid the nearby picnic table covered with bird droppings—and resisted the urge to pull off the oxford shoes that were killing my feet.

Killing. I pondered four of the obvious five W's about Cousin Will Ann's murder. Where was she killed, who put her body in our trunk, why put her in the place most designed to cast suspicion on us, and when did the murderer manage it?

Jack had carefully locked both the car and our large metal pole barn last night after completing his usual pre-contest, fine-tooth-comb inspection. Nothing appeared to be disturbed this morning at dawn when he drove his baby to the house to pick me up.

The what question struck me as being most important of all. As in what could we possibly do to convince the authorities that

11

neither of us was involved in this murder, despite the fact that we both had good reason to want my cousin Will Ann Lloyd dead?

CHAPTER TWO

I came awake with a jerk and swiped a bit of drool off my chin with the back of my fist. Jack was jiggling my shoulder. It took me a minute to shake off the nightmare and focus on what he was saying. That was when I realized it wasn't a nightmare after all. Several police officers surrounded the trunk of our car. The local coroner's black van was parked on the grass next to it, and someone was taking pictures. I hoped the roll of film didn't include a picture of me dozing under a tree.

I struggled to my feet and dusted the grass off my felt skirt. Jack gave me one of his lopsided grins. The kind that had won over my freshman heart the first time I'd set eyes on the cute new senior parked at the Blue Onion Drive In where I car-hopped for spending money. He'd been in a black '57 Chevy that night, borrowed, but eye-catching nonetheless. When he finally bought his own '57 many years later—after eons of searching through junk yards and corn fields—he'd painted this car the original color, Matador red. And christened her "Sadie," or "Sadie was a lady." Up until this morning she'd always behaved like a perfect lady, winning a trophy at every show Jack entered her in. The restoration was complete from the tuck-'n-roll headliner right down to her white walls. No power steering, of course, and certainly no air-conditioner, which made wearing those cute little sweater sets of mine a bit uncomfortable in mid-July.

A plainclothes officer walked over to us, loosened his tie, and flashed his badge.

"Mr. and Mrs. Bloodworth? I'm Detective Parker from the Paducah Police Department. I understand you own the vehicle in which the deceased was found?"

Deceased. Cousin Will Ann would've choked over that one, if she hadn't already been dead. I squared my shoulders. It was going to be a long morning. And hot.

The two males shook hands, ignoring me. "Yes, sir, it's our car."

"Tell me how you found the body?"

Jack pulled out a handkerchief and mopped his forehead. "We're members of the Metropolis Super Cruisers. Our club came over to Paducah to compete in this morning's contest. I propped open the hood for the judging, and went to unlock the trunk. That's when I found her."

Detective Parker jotted notes in the little book he'd pulled from his shirt pocket. I noticed he was left-handed. I also noticed the blue jay squawking in the tree limb just above my head, and the buzzing of the cicadas, and the murmur of the other car owners watching the scene from a safe distance. Truth be told, I was doing my best to notice everything except the two men lifting Cousin Will Ann's body out of our trunk. I came back into the conversation just in time to hear Jack volunteering us to break the news to her family.

"It would be much easier coming from us," he said.

No, it would not. It wouldn't be easier coming from anyone that I could think of. News like that was never easy. I gave Jack a small kick from under my voluminous skirt, but as usual, he was too quick for me.

"Now, then." Parker tapped the pen against his notebook. "Since the victim was found in your trunk, and you knew her well, I'll need a thorough account of your activities last night. Coroner estimates she's been dead about twelve hours. Where were you around eight o'clock last night?"

"Having dinner at Farley's Cafeteria, over near home in Metropolis, with the rest of the club." Jack pointed over his shoulder like he thought Parker could see through the trees clear across the Ohio River from where we stood. "We were finalizing plans for today's gathering. Our car club is hosting the competition."

"What time did you get to the restaurant?" Parker looked Jack up and down like he wasn't prepared to believe anything he said. I was getting nervous. He couldn't possibly think either one of us killed her.

"We arrived there about seven and left at ten. We ate dinner and discussed club business," Jack said. I watched as damp rings spread out underneath his armpits. His jacket was still tossed over his shoulder.

"So you both attended the meeting?"

"Yes, sir. I'm vice-president, and my wife is club treasurer. I was in charge of setting things up this morning. That's why we got here so early. Judging doesn't start until eight."

"When did you last see Mrs. Lloyd?"

Jack and I exchanged glances. We stumbled over each other verbally for a few sentences. Then I stepped in.

"She came to Farley's looking for us last night. She wanted to ask me something."

I could almost see Parker's ears perk up. "And that something was?"

"She wanted to know where she could find our younger daughter, Sunny. Will Ann said she needed to talk to Sunny right away. Sunny lives in Carbondale. She's gone back to SIU to get her degree. She was spending the night at a friend's apartment, so I told Cousin Will Ann she'd have to catch her later."

I was babbling, but I couldn't seem to help it. I had to tell him that much. If not, the rest of the club members probably would.

"Why did she want to see your daughter?" Parker pointed his pen at me in what I could only describe as an accusing manner.

"She didn't say."

I drew myself up to my full five-foot, ten-inch height and gave Parker my very best "angry teacher" look. I was gratified to see his shoulders droop just the teensiest bit.

"Did the victim talk with anyone else? When did she leave? And with who?" Parker asked.

I didn't think this was the best time to give him a corrective "whom."

"She left immediately. Alone. I looked down the stairs and saw her Beemer pull out of the little alleyway beside Farley's. She must have parked it there before she came inside."

"And you haven't seen or talked to Mrs. Lloyd since?"

"No," Jack said. "We went home and straight to bed. Preparing for this competition has worn us all out." He gestured toward the other Cruisers whispering under the trees nearby.

"Any idea where the victim went after she left Farley's? Could she have driven up to Carbondale to see your daughter?"

"No," we said in unison. Jack finished the sentence, as he'd been doing for me practically since we'd first met. "My daughter called right after we got home to say she'd probably spend the rest of the weekend with her friend. I told her Cousin Will Ann was looking for her."

"Had your cousin gotten in touch with her? Did she say what she wanted?"

"No. Sunny said she'd catch up with Will Ann when she got back to her own apartment," Jack said.

Which was only a slight lie. What Sunny had actually said was, according to her father, "Let her catch me if she can." Then she'd hung up.

"Did anyone see you between the time you left the restaurant and arrived home?" Parker asked as he swatted at a mosquito.

Jack and I exchanged looks again. "I gassed up the car," Jack said, "at the BP on the bypass road near home. A couple of high school kids stopped to admire her. Likely they'll remember us."

"I'll jot down their names for you," I offered. Anything to convince him we weren't involved in the murder. "I taught them both when I subbed at Massac High a few months ago."

"You're a teacher?" Parker said.

"Retired, after thirty years on the firing line, but I still sub now and then to keep my hand in."

"And you, sir?" Parker turned to Jack.

"Retired farmer, spend most of my time working on my car." Jack glanced longingly at the Chevy. Parker followed his look.

"Did either of you have a reason to want Mrs. Lloyd dead?" Parker crossed his arms over his ample stomach, as if he didn't think he'd get a printable answer. I felt myself go cold. Jack's gaze bounced off me before he answered.

"Will Ann Lloyd wasn't the most popular woman in Massac County, but neither of us would kill her. Why would we?"

Aside from the fact that she'd marched into Farley's Cafeteria last night and announced to the entire car club that our darling daughter Sunny was a tramp and a sneak, I certainly couldn't think of a single reason.

17

CHAPTER THREE

Luckily, we'd been dining upstairs when Cousin Will Ann threw her little hissy-fit, so none of the other Farley's patrons had heard her. Now, if only the other members of our group were loyal enough not to repeat that embarrassing episode in detail. Will Ann Lloyd was none too popular with the Metropolis Super Cruisers ever since she'd been caught keying Philby Mason's antique Model T because he'd beat her to the only available parking spot in front of the bank. She'd paid for the damages but refused to apologize. Philby threatened to strangle her right then and there, but given that he was a half-foot shorter, fifty pounds lighter, and a couple of decades older than his nemesis, I couldn't really count him as a suspect. His wife Reva was even older and smaller. Ditto for most of the rest of the group, including Jack, in the smaller category. That left me.

Cousin Will Ann wasn't teensy by anyone's description. Tall, muscular, and drop-dead gorgeous in her youth, by middle age she'd stopped growing up and had begun growing out—way out. The speak-her-mind personality that had been so refreshing in her hey-day turned to pure poison as she'd become widowed, fat, and middle-aged, in that order. Her life hadn't been happy, despite two beautiful children and a newer, younger husband. She was apparently determined to see that no one else's life was, either. She'd had an unerring aim and went for any weakness she saw in others. The list of suspects would likely be legion. Including her family. And, worse, ours.

Jack was in the middle of telling Parker that we hadn't seen Hank Lloyd, Cousin Will Ann's second hubby last night or today. I decided I'd had enough of Detective Parker's questions and feigned a fainting spell. I wasn't born in the forties for nothing. I'd watched enough noir films to know when the cops were moving in for the kill and when the heroine should fade out.

"Can my wife please sit down somewhere more comfortable?" Jack asked, cradling me against his shoulder. "This has been mighty tough on her."

Unless I missed my guess, it was going to get a lot tougher, and not just on me.

Parker nodded. Jack took my arm and led me over to Gene Hosman's green '52 Studebaker. Brand new in the group, Gene hadn't entered today's competition, so he probably wouldn't mind me sitting in it. As I slid onto the cool back seat, Parker called out that he'd be talking to us again. Soon. I could hardly wait.

"And I'll speak to the victim's husband and children myself, Mr. Bloodworth. I have some questions for them. But your offer is appreciated."

I hadn't appreciated Jack's offer. The last thing I wanted to do was tell Cousin Will Ann's husband and children that someone had offed her.

As soon as we arrived home, I tried calling our girls to break the news. Talking to Maggie was always a challenge with two kids yelling, dog barking, and television blaring in the background. I wished for the millionth time that my oldest daughter would send the kids to their rooms, throw the dog outside where she belonged, and turn off the TV. That probably wasn't going to happen.

"Cousin Will Ann's dead? Tori, stop that! What happened to

her? Car accident? If that dog throws up in here again, you'll be cleaning it up. When is the funeral? Billy, take that garden snake back outside and turn it loose this instant, then go to your room."

"Honey, there's no polite way to say this. Cousin Will Ann was murdered, and someone hid her body in Sadie's trunk. We found her this morning when your dad opened it for the judging."

"Tori, put Daisy outside. What? Mother, you can't be serious. Nobody would fool with Dad's old Chevy. Not if they wanted to go on living. Oh, dear, maybe that's just what happened?"

I shoved my cold cup of Chamomile tea into the microwave and set the timer for thirty seconds.

"Of course that's not what happened. Despite your father's frequent threats, he wouldn't have strangled Cousin Will Ann. Besides, she'd have whacked him upside the head or kicked his shins if he'd tried. This had to be someone much stronger than she was." The microwave dinged.

"Where was Cousin Hank? I know he was crazy about her, but the husband is always the first suspect and—" A crash interrupted Maggie. "Hang on, I've got to find out what that was."

It sounded to me like a kitchen wall had caved in at her house. Not totally beyond the realm of possibilities. I sipped my tea and waited. Scheherazade leaped onto my lap and sniffed at my cup. I rubbed her soft black fur, but a nip on my fingers let me know that wasn't what she was after. She sniffed at my cup again. I was pretty sure she preferred milk to tea, so I reached for the carton in the fridge, poured some in her bowl, and placed it on the floor. A soft "meow" was my thanks.

"Daisy lunged at the counter to get Tori's hot dog and knocked my favorite mixing bowl off. I put both of them outside. Honestly, Mom, I don't know what I'm going to do with these kids."

I resisted the urge to suggest a good old-fashioned spanking—the kind she'd been raised on and never injured by.

"I agree, Cousin Hank wouldn't hurt Cousin Will Ann," I said. "Heaven only knows why, but he adored her. I'm sure he'll take this very hard." I pulled the rubber band out of my hair, not caring if some hair came with it, and rubbed the spot where my head ached.

"So will her kids. At least Craig will. I don't know about Patricia Ann," Maggie said. "Guess we'd better get some food together and take it over there. I'll make a cold cornbread salad. Cousin Craig loves it. And I can fix a green bean casserole. Would you mind doing the meat?" I fumbled in the basket on the counter for my headache tablets, shook the bottle, and found it empty. Why couldn't Jack just tell me when we were out of something in the kitchen instead of sticking empty bottles or jars back in their place for me to find when it was too late?

"I'll fix a chicken casserole and bake a couple of pies. What time will you be free to go over there?"

"Joe should be home around five. Let me feed him and the kids, and then I'll pick you up. He can baby-sit."

Maggie was a stay-at-home mom, something I wish we could've afforded when our children were small. I was happy that she and Joe were able to live comfortably on his salary from the nearby plant where he worked as a foreman.

"I'll be ready."

But first I was going to get out of these ridiculous clothes and find something to take for my pounding head. Normally I loved wearing my poodle skirt. It made me feel like I was back in those wonderful days when Jack and I hung out at the Blue Onion, drinking Coke floats, and planning our future. We thought we had the world by the tail. It took a few years and a couple of kids to realize it was the other way around. But right now the outfit reminded me of Cousin Will Ann's body stuffed in the trunk of our car. Her eyes open and staring up at me, as if she couldn't believe someone had finally one-upped her.

Chapter Four

Shower over, hair neatly tied back, exercise jerseys enveloping me like a soft blanket, I headed into the kitchen and dug the ingredients out of the pantry for the casserole. It was one of my favorites, canned chopped chicken, mayo, cream of chicken soup, and potato chips crumbled on top. It wasn't Jack's favorite casserole—he was a roast and potatoes guy—so I generally saved it for when company came to dinner. He was too polite to fuss in front of them. Sneaky? Yes. I'd learned it at my mother's knee.

Which reminded me. What had Cousin Will Ann meant about my Sunny being a tramp and sneak? Of course I'd taught her and her sister most of a woman's basic survival tips, but certainly nothing that would have harmed another woman or set Cousin Will Ann off like a bottle rocket. What had the woman been babbling about last night?

I'd tried to call Sunny before my shower but got her voice mail. Voice mail. Cell phones. Must be nice to be able to talk to people while riding in a car or shopping at Wal-Mart. A lot of people considered cell phones intrusive, and I suppose they were in a restaurant or theater, but I'd wanted one for ages. For emergencies, if nothing else. But Jack hated modern technology. Of course we had a television, because they showed every kind of ball game known to man, not to mention a lot of other sports that weren't even sports. Street luge? Give me a break.

I popped the casserole into the oven and reached in the

freezer for a couple of pie crusts. I thawed them and pinched the edges to look home-made. Jack thought I still rolled my own crusts, but my momma hadn't raised a dummy. A can opener had long ago replaced the apple peeler, and in no time I had two pies in the oven alongside the casserole. I set the timer and plopped on the old couch in the den. Might as well relax for a few minutes. I turned on the television to see if there was any news about the murder. Schadzie took her station on the back of the couch where she could see out the window and keep an eye on me at the same time.

The timer woke me thirty-five minutes later, and I leaped up to check on the food. The casserole was bubbling, and the pies were golden-brown. I still had to fix Jack's supper, so I thawed a couple of hamburger patties and put them in the skillet. I figured I might as well fry up some frozen potatoes while I was at it. I poked my head into the refrigerator. No lettuce, but some sliced onion and a tomato or two, fresh from the garden, would top the burgers off perfectly.

Jack had been sulking in the garage ever since we'd gotten home. The huge pole barn was where he kept not only his beloved Sadie but loads of collectibles, including a couple of ancient gas pumps. It was obscene the price those things went for.

Detective Parker had ordered Jack to stay away from the pole barn while the crime scene technicians sent down from Carbondale went over it inch by inch. The three of them looked like something out of a B-grade fifties science fiction movie as they moved in and out of the huge doors. As I watched through my kitchen window, I prayed they'd find out how the killer managed to get into our barn, and Sadie's trunk, in order to dump Cousin Will Ann's body. As long as it didn't involve anyone we knew and loved.

The police had towed the Chevy away at the park, with Jack

watching every move the tow-truck operator made, and I swear I saw him swipe away a tear when Sadie disappeared beyond the stone entrance at Noble Park.

I was pouring iced tea into our glasses when he stepped into the kitchen, hung his baseball cap on the peg by the back door, and sniffed the air.

"Apple pie?"

"Yes. Maggie and I are taking food to Cousin Hank and the kids. I haven't been able to get in touch with Sunny. She isn't answering her cell phone, and her buddy Janet isn't home."

"Told you, cell phones are a government conspiracy to keep an eye on us. Doesn't do her a whole lot of good to have one if she doesn't answer it." He plopped into his favorite chair and scooted it up to the table.

I let the comment pass and reached for the catsup. Jack was silent through most of dinner, not like him at all. And I knew it wasn't about the Chevy.

"You're thinking about last night, aren't you?" I asked. "You practically lied to that detective this morning."

"I didn't lie. I just didn't tell him everything."

"Like how Cousin Will Ann stormed into Farley's Cafeteria last night and made accusations about our daughter?"

"I figured we should talk to Sunny first and find out what was going on." He shrugged and reached for the mustard. "Besides, you didn't tell him either."

Nor was I going to, rubber hoses or bright lights notwithstanding. Of course, modern police departments didn't use those methods nowadays. Instead, a cop would make the suspect think they were best buddies—exhibiting all understanding and friendliness—until said suspect, overcome with the warm-fuzzies, spilled his guts. I'm no novice. I watch Cops. It would take a lot more than Parker's warm-fuzzies to get me to rat out my baby daughter.

"What in the world do you suppose Will Ann meant?" Jack interrupted my courage-mustering.

"Well, maybe it had something to do with her baby boy, Craig. He and Sunny signed up for some of the same summer classes, and they've been studying together a whole lot. I suppose Cousin Will Ann thought more was going on." I twirled a now-cool French fry in the catsup. "Will Ann was pretty old-fashioned. She wouldn't have liked it if her son was dating our daughter."

Jack snorted. "Of all the—that's the dumbest thing I've ever heard. In the first place, Will Ann's mother and your mother were first cousins, so you and she were second cousins, or first cousins once removed—I can never keep that straight—and in the last place, Will Ann was adopted, so any possible blood relationship between Sunny and Craig would be non-existent."

"I know that, and you know that," I said, "but Cousin Will Ann wouldn't have cared. What other people thought was her major concern. Nothing mattered in life to her so much as putting up a proper appearance. She even refused to acknowledge that she was adopted."

"No use worrying about that now. Give Sunny another call and see if you can find out what's going on."

I wiped my hands on a paper towel and reached for the phone. This time Sunny answered. I filled her in on what had happened that morning.

"Mom, I can't believe it. Who would kill her? Never mind, just tell me who wouldn't." My younger child was not one to pull punches.

Neither was I. "Honey, where were you last night? The police are going to want to know."

"Where was she last night?" Jack whispered.

"Me? I was studying alone at Janet's apartment. I spent the night there. Like I told you when I called last night. Janet had a late date, and I was too tired to drive home. C'mon, Mom, you know I'm not the violent type. I don't even support capital punishment."

And when had she made that decision? I was again reminded of how quickly children grew up.

I took a deep breath. "Your father and I had dinner with the car club at Farley's last night. Cousin Will Ann blew in like last year's killer tornado and demanded to know where you were. I didn't tell her, of course. I said she'd have to call you. Did she try, by the way? Did you talk to her?"

"What did Will Ann want?" Jack asked, his voice slightly louder.

"Me talk to her? No. I accidentally let the cell phone battery run down yesterday, so it's been on the charger," Sunny said. "I forgot to take it to the library with me this morning. Did Cousin Will Ann say what she wanted with me?"

Jack was signaling me with a French fry. "Did Will Ann say what she wanted with Sunny?"

"I can't hear both of you, Jack." I was rarely able to hold a simple phone conversation whenever he was around without having to listen to and answer him at the same time.

"She only said she needed to talk to you immediately," I told Sunny. "Then she spun around and stomped off with her usual dramatic flair. She did manage to call you a tramp and a sneak before she flounced down the stairs."

Sunny made a choking noise in my ear.

"Any idea why she'd refer to you that way, honey? Of all our family, Cousin Will Ann has always been most tolerant of you. What would change her mind? Is there something I need to know? Before the police find out?"

Silence from the other end of the phone.

"What did Sunny say?" Jack asked. I threw a French fry at him.

"Sunny?"

"Cousin Will Ann doesn't . . . I mean didn't like my friendship with Craig, Mom. She's been all over him about it. But, honest, Craig and I are just friends. He's been a huge help in my classes."

At the ripe old age of twenty-five, Sunny had gone back to SIU to study pre-law, having decided being a clerk in a local attorney's office wasn't fulfilling enough. She wanted to try the cases in court herself. Craig was still figuring out what his major should be, after changing it several times, which, of course, had driven his mother crazy. Taking courses this summer was a way for them to graduate sooner.

"Besides, it isn't like we're really related, is it?" Sunny added.

I could almost see her biting her nails. Something definitely was going on. I'd just have to get to the bottom of it.

A horn honked, and I told Sunny I had to hang up. "Maggie and I are taking food to Cousin Hank's house. I'm sure Craig and Patricia Ann will be there by now. I'm anxious to hear what the police told them. Cousin Will Ann's family is bound to come under suspicion."

"Well, it wasn't Craig. He was studying with me."

I felt my ears shoot straight up into points, like Mr. Spock. "But you just said you studied at Janet's alone."

"No, Mom. I said Craig and I studied there together. Janet was gone. You must've not heard me, with Dad interrupting like always."

But her dad hadn't been interrupting at that particular moment, and I knew what I'd heard. My daughter had lied to me. But why? To protect whom? Herself? Or Craig? I'd certainly have to find that out.

"Kitty, Maggie says hurry up," Jack said from the back doorway. "She's low on gas and can't keep the van running very long."

I bid my younger daughter goodbye, grabbed the basket with the casserole and pie tucked inside, gave Jack a peck on the forehead, and headed out the door. He called after me, "Get gas at the station on Tenth, they dropped their prices today. And be careful!"

Like I was planning to have a wreck? Why did people always say that? And what was my younger daughter hiding?

CHAPTER FIVE

Maggie's red van slid to a stop in front of the Lloyds' home. She backed up, curbed it, and narrowly missed the fire hydrant at the edge of the driveway. Then she dropped the tire back down onto the pavement and turned off the engine. I released my death-grip on the arm rest and opened the door.

Whatever had possessed me to let her father teach her to drive, I couldn't rightly say. After all, I'd been the one to ride shotgun for most—if not all—of Jack Bloodworth's youthful drag races. He still held the unofficial county record for traversing the distance between Massac County High School and Memorial Gardens Cemetery in just under two minutes. A record that wasn't likely to be broken any time soon.

Maggie didn't so much tailgate other drivers as she downdrafted them, gaining maximum speed from their air flow. Stop signs were pause signs to her, and parking spaces easily became bumper car arenas. I reached for my basket, hoping I wasn't now carrying an apple casserole and a chicken pie.

Craig met us at the door.

"Cousin Kitty, Cousin Maggie, am I glad to see you! A detective is here, talking to Hank. Patricia Ann is throwing one of her usual fits, demanding to see a lawyer, and nobody's even accused her of anything."

Craig's dimples tugged at my heart, as they'd done since he was a baby. Lucky for him, Craig Tanner had inherited his mother's looks and muscular build and his late father's genteel personality. I wondered for the millionth time if Pete Tanner's car had really faltered on that railroad crossing, or if he'd deliberately stopped there in order to achieve the ultimate escape from his overbearing wife.

Maggie and I followed Craig into the living room. Patricia Ann jumped up and threw herself at my chest, sobbing and wailing. Maggie winked at me over Patricia Ann's spiky hairdo and pulled the basket out of my hand.

"I'll just put the food in the fridge. Don't want it to spoil, do we?"

I patted ineffectually at Patricia Ann's thin shoulder, wondering whether she was truly grieving the mother with whom she'd never gotten along or convincing the detective she wouldn't hurt a single dyed hair on the poor deceased's head. She wasn't fooling me. The opposite of her brother, Patricia Ann had her father's long, lanky figure and her mother's hair-trigger temper. Putting those two women together at any family gathering was akin to throwing gasoline on a fire, except it was more likely that innocent bystanders would get burned.

Maggie returned to the living room, gently peeled Patricia Ann off me, and guided her to the overstuffed beige couch—the same couch Cousin Will Ann had used when her kids were little. She'd removed the plastic cover at Hank's insistence when he'd married into the family, so I still couldn't figure out how she'd kept it so spotless all these years. Maybe she had the power to order stains around like she had her family?

Detective Parker said he was happy to see me. I nodded, unable to return the sentiment. I sat in the rocking chair near the fireplace. Maggie sat on the couch between Craig and Patricia Ann. Hank stood on the other side of the fireplace and filled his pipe. I noticed his hands shook, and his eyelids appeared to be swollen.

"Mrs. Bloodworth, I've been trying to locate your daughters

all day." Parker looked at me like he thought I'd been hiding them in my basement or something. "Every time I reached Mrs. Jamison's home number, I'd hear a child giggling and then the phone would go dead. I'd planned on dropping by there after my visit here, but you've saved me a trip."

"That was probably Billy," Maggie said. "He's two and has just learned to answer the phone, so we don't get a lot of our calls any more. He screens them for us."

"Where were you and your family last night, Mrs. Jamison? Can you account for your time all evening? Particularly around eight-thirty? That's about the last time Mrs. Lloyd was seen alive, and the coroner believes she died well before nine."

Maggie twirled an auburn curl while she pretended to think it over. She knew exactly where she was last night. She was just stringing Parker along. I knew I should have spanked her more often when I'd had the chance. On the other hand, I was glad someone found humor in this disaster.

"My family and I were at our daughter's soccer team fund-raiser dinner," she said, giving Parker her most innocent look. "Coach rented the Community Center for it. I was in charge of the meal, so I got there at five, and we didn't leave until well after ten. Some friends stayed and helped us clean up. The pots and pans are still in the back of my van, if you'd like to check."

So that's what the clanging noise had been. I'd thought she had a loose wheel. I should've known.

Parker turned his charm on me. "I've tried the number you gave me for your other daughter's cell phone. I keep getting her voice mail, and she hasn't returned my messages."

"I spoke to her just before we came here." I glanced at Craig. "Sunny said she was studying with Craig last night in Carbondale. She said he left quite late." Did I imagine it, or had Craig just turned pale?

"Yes," Craig said, "that's right. Sun and I did study together

32

last night. She has a very important test next week. I was quizzing her on the chapters."

Sun? They'd reached the nickname stage? This was more serious than I'd thought. I saw Maggie's eyebrows go up. Not much got past her.

Parker stood. "Well, that takes care of just about all of you," he said.

I glanced at Hank, and Parker followed my gaze. "Mr. Lloyd was at the Metropolis Chamber of Commerce meeting between the hours of seven and ten. It is close enough to Farley's for him to have walked there, but the other members at the meeting don't remember him leaving the room at any time."

"That's correct," Hank said. "Last month's Superman Celebration was a huge success. It drew the largest crowd in history. So we're now deep in the planning stages for next year's festivities, but I doubt I'll be able to carry on after what's happened to my wife." He studied the Persian rug under his feet.

As the only Metropolis listed in the U. S. zip code book, our small town was dubbed the "Home of Superman" by the Illinois state legislators way back in the seventies. Our *Planet* newspaper, our large chunk of kryptonite plunked down on a busy street corner, and our fifteen-foot-tall Superman statue guarding the courthouse lured tourists from all over the world. Hank, as chamber president, had been in charge of this year's festivities.

"And you, Mrs. Bloodworth," Parker continued. "You said you saw your cousin driving out of the alleyway when she left the restaurant at about eight-thirty. Is that right?"

I nodded and watched Parker's belly bounce up and down as he ticked off the alibis for the rest of the suspects. Hubby and I at Farley's Cafeteria. Maggie at the Community Center with her family. Sunny and Craig in Carbondale, over an hour away.

Patricia Ann worked for the local television station across the river in Paducah as a sports reporter and had been seen by several thousand area residents as she gave her nightly report of a hotly contested high school tournament. She'd coached girl's basketball for many years until the station lured her away with more money and no teenage girls to deal with. The station was too far away for her to attack her mother any time before ten-thirty. So much for family suspects. That, at least, was good news. But what was Craig hiding? Was Sunny covering for him? Him for her? Each for the other? I was dizzy with the possibilities.

CHAPTER SIX

The early morning sun shot through the bedroom window straight into my eyes. One of these days I was going to have to get heavier curtains. I turned over and reached for Jack. He wasn't there. He'd been doing that a lot lately—sliding quietly away before I woke up. No sound from the television, so he must be in his garage again. Probably cleaning. Or building the shelves he'd been promising me for several months.

I felt my way to the kitchen, only tripping over the cat once, getting hissed at for my clumsiness. As I reached for the coffee pot, I saw that I was in luck. Jack had made a full pot before going to the garage. Might as well fire up the computer while I waited for my eyes to open all the way.

I fumbled my way out to the large sun porch at the back of the house and set my cup on the desk. Scheherazade, in a forgiving mood for a change, jumped onto my lap and settled in after exercising her claws on my bathrobe. I practically lived on this porch, using the house mostly to shower, sleep, or take care of those pesky household chores. The rest of my at-home time was spent out here, playing with our grandchildren, reading, surfing the Internet, or watching the birds fight over the feeders hanging from the trees just outside the huge windows that took up most of the wall space.

Jack had added the porch behind the kitchen as his twenty-fifth wedding anniversary gift to me. Might not sound like a romantic gift, but it was. I could open the windows in almost any weather to take advantage of the breezes, and in winter, with the windows shut and the ceramic heater humming, I was nice and toasty. So were the herb container plants I raised year round. And, of course, one fat, lazy cat.

I glanced through the windows, relieved to see that the crime scene technicians hadn't arrived as yet to take over Jack's huge barn again. Just to the left of the barn, the surface of the old pond was smooth, undisturbed by the pigs that used to drink or cool off in there. Now only the frogs and insects made use of it, and an occasional snake.

I took a gulp of coffee and clicked into my email account. Terrific, I couldn't get in. Password wasn't working. I tried it again. Still no luck. What had I done wrong this time? There was a good reason that little blinking thing was called a cursor. That's what it usually made me want to do.

Well, if I couldn't go in through the front door, I might as well try the account I'd set up for Jack to do his eBay thing. I could pull my e-mail into there. Maybe.

Thirty minutes later my coffee was gone, my eyes were fully functioning, and I'd posted the list of the five most humorous mysteries I'd ever read on a book discussion group. I loved chatting on the Internet with other mystery readers, seeing which books got a thumb's up or down. I'd also sent Aunt Dilly the recipe she needed, and read my quota of e-jokes for the day.

I deleted all my mail so Jack wouldn't know I'd been in his account—no use stirring up trouble—and was about to click out when a name caught my eye. Doctor Morrison. Why would Jack be receiving an e-mail from a well-known Paducah surgeon? He hated going to the doctor. I usually had to make his appointments, toss him over my shoulder, and haul him in for a checkup.

Maybe I should read it. No. I wouldn't want him reading my e-mails, even though there wasn't anything sensitive in them. It was the principle of the thing. Married couples had to have some areas of privacy. If all were revealed, things could get boring. Particularly after forty-some-odd years.

But why an e-mail from a specialist over in Paducah rather than our family doctor right here in Metropolis? Maybe Jack would tell me later, when things calmed down over Cousin Will Ann's murder.

I swear I pointed the arrow straight at the "close" button, but somehow that e-mail just popped right open. And I couldn't help seeing that it was a reminder for an appointment Jack had made with Dr. Morrison's office for next week. Despite the coffee, the large cat on my lap, and my fuzzy robe, I suddenly felt cold. Why was Jack seeing Dr. Morrison, on his own, without telling me, and worse, without any nagging from me? Various possibilities leaped to mind, none pleasant.

I shut down the computer, placed the cat in her basket, and headed for the garage door. Might as well tackle Jack right now. I've never been known for my patience.

Wait. If I asked, he'd know I'd looked at his e-mail. And he'd be mad. Never a nosy person, he respected the privacy of others and expected the same in return. I'd have to find out what the e-mail was about some other way. By just waiting for him to come clean? That could take eons, and I wasn't good at waiting.

There was more than one way to skin a cat, as my momma always said. I glanced apologetically at the fat fur ball in the basket. Momma always said you just needed the right knife and the right end of the cat. I changed back into the exercise jerseys I'd worn last night, grabbed my keys, and walked into the garage. Jack sat with his back to the door, fiddling with something at his workbench.

"Jack, I'm going to the Senior Center for aerobics class." And to ask some questions. "Want anything while I'm out?"

"Nothing I can think of." He put down the level, strolled

over, reached up, and gave me a half-hearted peck on the cheek.

"Are you okay, honey?"

"Just ducky, thanks," he said, "and you?"

"What's going on?"

"Nothing. I'm having trouble getting this shelf leveled up, that's all. Thought this would be a good time to work in here, since the police sealed off my pole barn yesterday. No telling when they'll let me back in. Parker thinks the killer sneaked her body out there and put it in the trunk after I'd locked up for the night. He hasn't figured out how, yet, since I have the only key."

Great, one more nail in our coffin.

"Talk to the girls this morning?" Jack asked.

"Not yet. I'll check in with them when I get home. I figured I'd better go to class and work off some of Farley's homemade pie." I stepped back and stared down at him. He looked as if he hadn't slept in a month. I dropped my purse on a stool.

"Detective Parker can't possibly think you killed Cousin Will Ann," I said. "For one thing, you couldn't have reached her neck without a step ladder." Jack hated any reference to his lack of stature, but this wasn't the time for polite denial.

"I pointed that out to Parker. I'm not sure he buys it. Can't say I blame him, given the number of things to stand on and reach within the pole barn."

"You were with me and the rest of the club when Cousin Will Ann died. He can't prove any different. What else is bothering you?"

Jack shrugged. "Nothing. I didn't sleep well."

Big surprise. "Look, you fixed that Chevy up once, you can fix her again, when we get her home. I'm sure they'll take great care examining her." I didn't know that for certain, but I wanted to reassure Jack.

He locked gazes with me. "I'm selling Sadie as soon as they

release her. You don't seriously think I could keep her?"

My heart bounced off my tennis shoes. "Jack, you spent eight years restoring that car. You love her almost as much as you love me and the girls. You can't sell her."

"I can't keep her. Sadie is only a car. I'll find something else to do."

Only a car? I scrounged for a quick argument. "Okay. You've been promising me a street rod for as long as I can remember. Why not put Sadie in moth balls for a while, and we'll work on a new project together?"

He shook his head. "I'll probably drop out of the club as well." He turned back to the balky shelf and examined it.

Drop out of the antique car club? Most, if not all, of his high school buddies were members of that group. They were known at the local Hardee's as the Romeos—Really Old Men Eating Out. What would he do without them? Shrivel up and die, most likely.

I didn't want to think about that. I grabbed my purse and headed to Beetle, my ancient VW. I'd give Jack some time to think this all over. No use pushing the issue right now. Besides, he'd need my signature on the pink slip to sell the Chevy, and he wasn't getting it. Not without a fight.

CHAPTER SEVEN

I squeezed Beetle into a parking space between Ellen Carter's thirties black roadster and Betty Adler's huge ancient yellow Caddy, trying not to drool over their respective classics. Practically all the other members of the car club had bought and restored second vehicles for their wives to drive. My little Volkswagen was built in the early sixties and still chugged along better than the current models, but Jack had promised me one of those fabulous forties numbers—complete with suicide doors. We hadn't found one in our price range. Yet.

My best friend, Debby, was already stretching when I took my place beside her. "Heard about Will Ann. I called you last night, but Jack said you were taking food to her family. I took something over this morning. And I have a casserole in my trunk for you. I didn't think you'd feel much like cooking right now."

"Thanks." I did some deep knee bends and struggled to stand straight again. I was already sweating and we hadn't even started.

"How are you and Jack holding up? I can't imagine what you're going through. I mean, I know you and Will Ann weren't close, but this has to be pretty awful for you. Can I do anything?"

I burst into tears. Debby stopped stretching and gave me a hug. A couple of the other exercisers gathered 'round, clucking, tisking and hugging. The shock of Cousin Will Ann's murder had worn off and I was ready to grieve.

After a few body-shaking sobs, I dried my eyes and took a

deep breath. "We hadn't been close, and I'm not a hypocrite, but Cousin Will Ann was a big part of my early childhood. I idolized her before I found out what she was really like. Now she's gone . . . one of the few people who still remembered bare feet on cool grass, or making tea cups out of fallen leaves for a spur-of-the-moment party."

The girls nodded.

"She even gave me some of her paper dolls when she outgrew them. I still have them in a drawer, tucked away in tissue paper. She hinted they were probably worth a small fortune on an Internet auction and said I was a dope for hanging on to them for Tori."

"Don't blame you for keeping them," Betty said. "They don't even make paper dolls anymore, do they? Times change, and not always for the better. I always kept my paper dolls in those neat little boxes my mother's nylon stockings came in."

"Thank goodness we don't have to wear those any more," Debby said. "I could never keep the seams straight."

I smiled at that because I'd never been able to keep them straight either.

Shirley Mumfort, the exercise maven, asked if I'd like to come back another day.

"No, I need to sweat this out. I'm fine now." Actually, in that huge wall mirror, I looked like Lot's wife. Frozen in place, paper white skin, bony frame. Dolly Parton had nothing to fear from me. I forced myself to start kicking with the music, all the while thinking. Who killed Cousin Will Ann, and why? How did she wind up in our trunk? And worse, was the killer someone I knew and loved?

I missed a move on the stepper and nearly lost my balance. I should give it a rest, but I wanted to talk to the girls after class. See if they knew anything about Cousin Will Ann, or about Jack's health. Most of their husbands were Romeos. Metropolis was a small town. Not much happened that everyone didn't hear about, often before it was reported in the *Planet*.

We opted for lunch at El Tequila. Might as well "stabilize" our metabolisms while we were at it. Deb sat on my right. It was great having a best friend who knew my every mood and gave support when needed. And she remembered I was left-handed and likely to elbow anyone on that side. As much as Jack loved me, he seldom remembered that. And female tears upset him to the point of disappearing into the garage or pole barn, fearing he couldn't solve the problem. Husbands were terrific for warming beds, repairing broken things, and keeping roofs over heads with money in the bank, but they weren't much punkin' with tears.

Water and coffee arrived, orders were taken, and we settled down to business. Time for me to bring up the subject we were all thinking about.

"Girls, Cousin Will Ann's family members, and mine, are obviously the first suspects. Jack is really upset by the whole thing. I want to figure out who killed her. The Paducah police are good, but . . ." I took a gulp of water. This was going to be harder than I thought. "Anybody know anything that would help?" I asked.

I saw glances exchanged around the table. They knew something. Etta Strong cleared her throat, taking her own sweet time about answering, as usual.

"Will Ann wanted to be Queen Mother of our Red Hat group," Etta said at last. "But none of us were that dumb." She sniffed and glanced around the table.

"We all met several days ago," she continued, "and cara-vanned down to Nashville for lunch and shopping at the Opry Mills mall. The other girls move faster than I do, and I had a lot of packages, so on the way home I got stuck in the back seat of Betty's Caddy with Will Ann." Etta blew a curl out of her eyes and shot Betty an accusing look.

I did wish Etta wouldn't die her hair jet-black. On the wrong side of eighty, she certainly wasn't fooling anyone about her age. And a smidge of brown or red would've at least made the color look more natural. Etta glanced over her shoulder, as if to make sure no one overheard. We all leaned forward.

"Will Ann pumped everyone in the car for information. She was sure Craig had a new girlfriend. She wanted to know if we'd seen anything." Etta leaned back in her chair. "Would you believe she wanted all of us to keep an eye on him? Even went so far as to suggest that some of us might follow him." Her har-rumph was followed by giggles and snorts.

Shirley Mumfort chimed in. "It's true. She did the same thing in my car on the way down." Shirley blushed. I knew what was coming.

"She thought Craig was dating my Sunny, didn't she?"

Shirley nodded. "She said she was going to put a stop to it before it created a scandal. As if it could. There's nothing wrong with those two dating, assuming they are."

I shrugged. "Sunny says they're just studying together. I believe her." For the most part.

Debby said, "Did Will Ann say what she'd do if they were dating? I mean, they're certainly both of age, and Craig is on a scholarship, so what could she do to stop them?"

Trust Deb to go to the heart of the matter. "I don't know," I said, "But knowing Cousin Will Ann, it wouldn't have been pretty."

"Do you suppose they'll let us play our kazoos at the funeral?" Ellen asked. "Like we did for Jenny, when she passed last year?"

My jaw dropped. I'd been out of town for Jenny's funeral. Had the girls really been allowed to play their kazoos? And had they actually showed up in purple and red? How had I missed hearing about that one?

"I suppose it's up to Hank," I said. "You'll have to ask him. I don't have anything to do with the funeral arrangements." Thank heaven.

Debby bumped me with her knee. "It was all very tasteful and it made me cry. I'm sure Hank wouldn't mind. Besides, I hate to say it, but it would make it look like Will Ann had a lot of friends, even though she didn't."

I choked on my coffee. Kazoos and Cousin Will Ann?

The girls gave me injured looks in stereo. They'd invited me several months ago to join the Metropolis Chapter of the Red Hat Society so I could celebrate growing older with them, participate in their lovely luncheon meetings, and learn to play the kazoo. And I'd agreed to join, just as soon as I stopped substitute teaching. During the school year I couldn't always get off long enough for daytime meetings, but I was dying to wear one of those huge hats.

Our orders arrived, and I thankfully tucked into my quesadilla.

It wasn't until I was on my way home that I remembered I'd forgotten to ask the girls if they'd heard anything about Jack needing to see the doctor. I'd have to do that soon.

CHAPTER EIGHT

Arriving at the edge of our long driveway, I pulled over to the wrong side of the road to check the contents of our ancient mailbox. Hopefully no spiders lurked inside the large metal box. Despite my frequent requests for him to do so, Jack still hadn't sprayed weed killer on the morning glory vines that kept the support post in a strangle-hold and made opening the mailbox cover difficult.

I took a gulp of fresh air, retrieved the bills, advertisements, and a package of books I'd ordered off the Internet, and bounced Beetle down our long gravel driveway, parking in front of the garage. The crime scene technicians surrounded Jack's pole barn again, looking for all the world like they were ready to smoke out a cattle rustler.

I went inside the house through the garage. No sign of Jack there. He wasn't in his favorite old leather chair in the living room either, though the ceiling fan was whirring and the television was tuned to his favorite sports channel. I picked up his discarded paper plate from the coffee table, carefully balancing his empty soda can on top, and headed to the kitchen, calling out his name. I finally spotted him from the sun porch, standing near the steps, hands on hips, chatting with one of the technicians about the many trophies that lined the shelves in the pole barn. I headed back into the kitchen.

I was staring inside the fridge, hoping something would materialize that would make a decent dinner, when Debby came in the back door.

"I forgot to give you this casserole at the gym." She set the cold-carry-all on the counter and unzipped it. "Mercy, there are enough guys out there in paper outfits to dust a gymnasium floor. Think they've found anything?"

I pulled two sodas out of the fridge and handed one to her. "I don't know. Part of me hopes so, the other part hopes not."

"Look, everybody knows neither you nor Jack would strangle Will Ann. Jack would've used a tire iron on her, and you, well, you'd just smack her into the middle of next week and tell her to 'shape up or ship out.' Mercy, remember how our charming basketball coach, old Healy-Monster used that same tired saying—'shape up or ship out'—every single time we missed a basket? He was such a cranky old guy."

She popped the top of the soda can and slurped the fizz. I must have jiggled that six-pack when I put it in the fridge. My soda bubbled over as well.

"Coach Healy was only in his mid-thirties, a mere baby, Deb."

"Well, he looked like Father Time to this freshman. He must be in a nursing home by now, assuming he's still alive. He's never been to any of our reunions." She took another slurp.

"One can only hope." I glanced out the open kitchen window again. One of the technicians stood in the driveway. He was ogling Debby's magnificent '63 turquoise Mustang. I heard him tell Jack he was dying to own a car like that. Poor choice of words. The rest of the techs appeared to be packing up to leave. Had they found anything that would solve this case and let us get back to normal?

I watched through the window as Jack strode toward the garage, head down. Even though he had his Romeo buddies, he wasn't one to share feelings. Not even with me. If this went on for months—and it well could—his ego was bound to suffer, not to mention his health. How could I help him through this?

I took a too large swig of cola and swallowed hard as the fizz burned its way up my throat to my nose. Debby handed me a paper towel. "Want me to have Leo talk to him? Find out how he's doing?"

It was time to spill my guts about my spying operation this morning and Jack's doctor's appointment, the one he'd somehow forgotten to mention. Debby knew me well. She wasn't shocked.

"Leo hasn't told me anything, but I'll see if he can talk to Jack," she offered. "I'll tell him to be discreet."

Leo Evans had all the discretion of an unpinned hand-grenade, but I was desperate to know what was going on. "Okay, thanks."

"Has he had any problems with . . . you know?" She shrugged. "S-E-X?"

Debby always spelled it out. Fifties upbringing. Warped an entire generation. "Of course not," I said. "We've never had a problem in that area."

She cocked an eyebrow at me. I pulled a metal stool from under the kitchen island and gestured for Debby to sit on the opposite side. She took the lid off the dancing pig cookie jar, peeked inside, and pulled out a ginger snap for each of us before taking her seat. Comfort food. I took a huge bite before answering her unspoken question.

"Okay, so we haven't been as close lately. I've had this awful cold and he's been tired, and . . ." Come to think of it, I couldn't remember the last time Jack had reached for me. We'd both been tired at night, and cranky with off-season sinus infections. Maybe it was time to lose the flannel and bring out the little lace number again. Assuming I could locate it where I'd hidden it from our grandkids. Not to mention our daughters.

"You never really answered my question this morning," Debby said.

47

I raised an eyebrow. My mind reading abilities seemed to have gone south.

"About Will Ann. And how you're handling all this."

"On a scale of one to ten, with ten being the best, I'd say I'm about a five. Like you said, we weren't close. But she was a large part of my childhood and I'll miss her. I guess I kept hoping she'd get nicer as she grew older. Instead, she got worse."

"People do that. Seems character traits we had as young people become more noticeable as we go through the aging process. Which is why I'm trying to be sweeter as I grow older. So my kids will come see me in the nursing home."

We shared a hug over that one. Nursing homes were fine for other people, but no one I knew actually looked forward to living in one. We all wanted to stay at home and maintain our independence as long as possible.

"I didn't want to say anything in front of the girls at lunch, but I'm afraid either Sunny or Craig is hiding something," I said.

"About Will Ann's murder?"

"You heard Cousin Will Ann accuse Sunny of being a tramp and a sneak at the car club meeting. Sunny says she has no idea what that was about, but I think she's lying. And from what the girls said today, Cousin Will Ann was obviously snooping around in Sunny's life. But that can't possibly have anything to do with the murder, can it?"

"Of course not," Debby said. "Even if she wanted to, Sunny could never strangle Will Ann. I'm thinking the police should be looking for an angry giant. No one else could have taken Will Ann Lloyd down. Not if she was in a fighting mood."

I nodded. Debby scrunched the soda can, then bounced it off the edge of my trash can and onto the floor. "Guess I'm a little out of practice." She retrieved the can and tossed again, making the shot this time, then slid back onto her stool. "Why do you suppose Will Ann was such a witch?" Debby asked. "Where did she get that humongous chip on her shoulder?"

"I don't know for sure. Maybe because of Uncle Will's sudden death. Or because of the way Aunt Ann reacted to it. Cousin Will Ann was a real 'daddy's girl.' Uncle Will had a heart attack when she was a very active five-year-old. Aunt Ann took to her bed for a whole year, and Uncle Will's parents pretty much raised Cousin Will Ann during that time. Momma said it was easier for them to let her have her way than to try to rein her in."

"She was adopted, right? Maybe that explains part of it. Who were her real parents?"

"Her mother was one of Uncle Will's patients. Her father died a few weeks before she was born, and her mother right after the birth. Influenza was bad that year. The baby somehow survived, and Uncle Will brought her home to raise."

"So you don't know what her real folks were like?"

"Aunt Ann said they were good people. There wasn't any other family left, so she and Uncle Will planned to raise Cousin Will Ann as their own."

"No telling what really shaped her, is there? Genetics, environment, peer pressure?"

"Personally, I've always thought it was all three that shaped people. Sunny is just as stubborn as my mother, and Mom was gone by the time Sunny was born. But once my mother made up her mind, she never changed it."

Debby snickered and pointed at me. "You can be a bit on the stubborn side when the occasion calls for it."

"Me, stubborn? Whatever are you talking about?" We laughed, and I felt a rush of relief. I'd been afraid I wouldn't be able to laugh again for a very long time.

I finished my soda and tossed the can. How brief life seemed. And when it was over, our bodies were put underground, leaving all of our dreams and plans unfinished. What had been Cousin Will Ann's dreams for the rest of her life? And had she been planning more mischief for our family?

CHAPTER NINE

"Fooey."

I should've filed that fingernail before it poked through my last pair of black pantyhose. I dug the clear nail polish out of the drawer, and placed it on my nightstand, quickly scooting the bottle out of the path of the lacy window curtains flapping in the early morning breeze. With any luck, the run in my pantyhose wouldn't spread too quickly for me to seal it off. I air dried my hasty repair job in front of the window, then wiggled and twisted my way into the control-tops, thankful for the technology that eliminated girdles and those little rubber snaps that always dug into the backs of a woman's legs.

"What am I wearing?" Jack held out four shirts and his entire necktie selection, all gifts from me or the girls because he refused to shop for his own clothes.

"This one." I pointed to the dark purple, long-sleeved shirt, and slid the matching tie off the rack and into his hand.

"What are you going to do when I'm gone?" I said. "Who's going to dress you then?"

He headed back to the bathroom without answering. We'd had this conversation before. Many times. Coming into the world in the forties had left a lot of male baby-boomers color challenged. Black suits and white shirts no longer cut it, and many older men were totally at sea about what colors matched what.

I slid into the basic black dress that only came out of the

closet for funerals. As I buttoned the last few buttons, it occurred to me that Jack hadn't tried to make a pass at me when I'd been struggling into my pantyhose. Hadn't even whistled. Nor had he risen to the lace-bait last night. Too tired, or so he'd said. Something was definitely wrong. But getting information out of Jack Bloodworth when he didn't want to give it was about as easy as pulling a snake backwards out of its hidey-hole, and, once you got it out, you probably weren't going to like the results.

I settled myself on the small bench in front of the vanity and brushed a couple of tangles out of my hair. No ponytail for me today, just a straight, smooth hairdo under a big black hat. When I was a little girl, my mother always insisted I brush my hair at least one hundred strokes each night to make it thick and shiny. Probably just an old wives tale, but my hair was thick and made my neck hot, hence the usual ponytail I wore. I suspected Will Ann's mother had insisted she use the same bedtime routine, because Will Ann's hair always looked perfect, not a stray lock anywhere. Well, at least not until the night she was murdered. I swallowed hard and reached for my favorite clip-on earrings.

"You ready?" Jack stood at the foot of our bed and checked his watch.

I was ready, but he wasn't, so I straightened his collar and buttoned the top of his shirt closed. He usually left it open underneath the tie, and I usually buttoned it for him because it looked so tacky the other way. I checked him over, but he wasn't meeting my gaze, so I picked up my purse and headed for the garage.

I've always hated funeral homes. The smells, the sounds. And all those tissue boxes placed on every available space.

I signed the guest book, wondering if grieving family members actually hung onto them. Or really ever read them after the funeral. Sunny waved at me from a pew in the back. Craig sat beside her. Interesting. Apparently Maggie wasn't here yet. I prayed she wouldn't bring the kids. With any luck, her mother-in-law would baby-sit them.

Jack reached for my hand and firmly guided me toward the casket. "Might as well get this over with," he said.

With a nod I glanced at the cards tied to the various flower arrangements against the wall. I spotted the very expensive spray of roses I'd sent for our family. Cousin Will Ann always loved roses, so it was the least I could do. Beside it loomed a huge red and purple hat created from chrysanthemums. Out of the corner of my eye, I could see two rows of women in purple dresses topped off with red hats. I wondered if Hank had agreed to the kazoos. This might be an interesting funeral after all.

Hank stood to the left of the casket, with Patricia Ann draped over his shoulder like a cheap fox stole. I gave them each a hug, squared my shoulders, and stepped over to the casket. I was not going to cry. I'd get through this. My jaw was beginning to ache.

"Doesn't Mother look wonderful? I can't believe how much younger she looks," Patricia Ann said at my elbow. She'd now draped herself all over me. I swallowed on the gag reflex and resisted the urge to turn and run screaming out of the place.

Far from wonderful, Cousin Will Ann looked like a thick bath towel that had been run through the old wringer washer I'd used the first year Jack and I were married. I was thankful the mortician had been able to cover the strangulation marks on her neck. Patricia Ann reached out and stroked her mother's face. I nearly wet my pants.

"I need to sit down." I disentangled myself and headed for the nearest family pew, practically tripping over Detective Parker en-route. He was probably hoping the guilty party would throw him or herself on the casket, weeping, and confess on the spot.

I grabbed a tissue out of the box on the seat, and covered my mouth and nose so I didn't have to smell the flowers. Next thing I knew, I was hunched over my knees, sobbing my guts out.

Whoever said funerals were "necessary for closure" was an idiot. Funerals left a bad taste—and smell—in the minds of the survivors and replaced their vision of a vital, living human being with an empty, useless, discarded shell. Not to mention the obvious reminder that we'd all be in the same position one day, no pun intended. Better we should bury the dead quickly, with respect, but without the usual long drawn-out ceremony.

I hiccupped to a stop, reached for more tissue, and found Jack sitting beside me. "It's almost time to start. You okay?"

I nodded. He squeezed my shoulder, knowing better than to invade my space at a time like this. I wasn't a delicate crier. I tended to make my distress known to anyone within a mile radius. Too much sympathy could raise that distance to two miles or better.

Thankfully, Cousin Will Ann had requested no wake, just a short service and a quick burial. But would our preacher comply? Some folks in the congregation said he could begin a sermon at winter solstice and still be going strong on vernal equinox. They didn't get any argument out of me.

"Is Maggie here?" I asked Jack.

"Yeah. She and Joe are in the back with Sunny. I tried to get them to move up here to the family pew, but Sunny said she wasn't up to it. Maggie's staying back there with her."

I shushed him. "The funeral director is getting ready to shut the casket." Craig, Hank, and Patricia Ann took their places on the pew in front of us.

As it turned out, I never did actually hear the sermon. Brother

Maxxum gave the eulogy, then sat down as the Red Hatters marched solemnly to the front, raised their kazoos, and did the most moving rendition of "Amazing Grace" I'd ever heard.

It was fabulous, but the sight of all that purple and red swaying to the beat was more than I could stand, and I fled down the side aisle to the little anteroom behind, struggling to keep my hoots and guffaws to a minimum.

I was more than a little afraid Cousin Will Ann would sit up in her coffin and demand they stop playing in the name of all that was sophisticated and snobbish. I laughed and I cried and I prayed, and by the end of the service I thought I might actually survive this whole fiasco.

At the cemetery—after a blessedly short prayer at the family vault—I pulled Jack toward Beetle. I couldn't abide closed-in, dark places, and no way was I standing there while they sealed that door. Give me cremation any day and scatter me in some lovely open space.

We arrived at the Lloyds' for the family gathering and I got busy helping Cousin Will Ann's Sunday School class serve the meal they'd so kindly provided. Keeping busy was better than standing around munching finger foods and discussing "the good old days." Maggie had left to pick up the kids, and Sunny and Craig stood in a corner, whispering together over cups of coffee. I glanced around the elegant room and saw Debby hovering nearby, helping with the serving and cleaning up chores. She winked as she gathered up a pile of discarded paper plates. Cousin Will Ann would've had a fit at the mere thought of a used paper plate invading her living room. Or any other part of her house, for that matter.

Cousin Hank again stood near the fireplace. As he filled his pipe, he chatted with Ellen Carter and Betty Adler. Every time Ellen punctuated a sentence with a toss of her head, the huge purple feather in her hat swiped Hank's cheek. He didn't look annoyed. Probably too deep in grief.

Hank had a solid alibi, via the entire board of the Chamber of Commerce, but Farley's was practically next door. Could he have somehow managed to slip over there and attack Cousin Will Ann in the alleyway? And if so, why? And why were Craig and Sunny giving each other an alibi? Which one needed it? Certainly not my eldest daughter, Maggie. Strangulation wouldn't be her murder weapon of choice. Her van would.

Jack came up behind me, and gave me a hug. "You okay?"

"I'll be fine," I whispered. "I had a good cry and a good laugh at the funeral home."

"Happy to hear it," he said. "We've never known a murder victim before. I know you two weren't close, but this can't be easy for you. Underneath it all, despite Will Ann's obnoxious behavior to everyone, you cared about her."

I didn't dare answer that or I might start bawling again. I already looked like a blistered marshmallow. And besides grieving for Cousin Will Ann, I had the very real worry about whether or not someone I loved had killed her and stuffed her into our Chevy trunk. I couldn't imagine who would do that, friend or foe. Naturally, I preferred foe.

CHAPTER TEN

Jack asked, "What are you doing up so early?" Generally he beat me to the bathroom.

"Patricia Ann asked me to help sort through and dispose of some of her mother's things."

Belching and scratching, Jack swung his legs over the edge of the bed and shuffled toward the bathroom, his hair reminiscent of the Gerber Baby. He wasn't at his most charming first thing in the morning. To be perfectly honest, neither was I.

"Isn't it a bit soon?" Jack asked. "We just put Will Ann in the family vault yesterday. Don't they say wait a few months before making major changes or decisions?"

If he said anything else, the sound of the toilet flushing drowned it out. Entering the bathroom, I pulled my toothbrush out of the holder and reached for the toothpaste. "Patricia Ann insisted that her mother's things be sorted and divided up immediately. She has a copy of Cousin Will Ann's last will and testament, giving all her personal belongings to her children. Jewelry, furs, things like that. Hank keeps the house and the Beemer. And the furniture, except for family heirlooms. Those go to the kids as well."

Jack peered into the mirror, as if hoping what he saw would magically be replaced by something that looked human.

"Yeah, but why the rush? Everything will still be there in a month or so, right?"

"Of course it will, but you know Patricia Ann. Subtle as a

steamroller and just as effective when she wants her own way. I think she's afraid Hank will sell everything at a yard sale and run off to Tahiti or something."

"He'd best not run off too soon," Jack said. "Not while the investigation is still going on. Alibi or no, that wouldn't look good."

He grabbed a towel and headed into the shower, without his usual attempt to make a pass at me and without switching on the overhead fan. The bathroom quickly filled with steam. I knew Jack was upset about Cousin Will Ann's murder, and the possibility of someone we knew being found guilty. Still, it just wasn't like him. Even after forty years, he rarely passed by me without a pat or a squeeze. I had to find some way to pry loose whatever was bothering him.

I finished dressing, fed Schadzie, grabbed a cup of tea and a piece of toast topped with peanut butter and honey, and headed to my bug.

Five minutes later I pulled into the Lloyds' driveway, with tea stains on my jeans and honey dripping off my thumb. I reached for the Wipes in the glove box and cleaned myself up as best I could. Patricia Ann met me at the door.

"Hank insists on being here. I told him it wasn't at all necessary, but I think he's afraid we'll make off with the refrigerator or something." She glanced at Beetle, as if speculating whether or not said refrigerator would fit in the trunk. I'd been known to get quite a lot in there, but my Volkswagen did have its limits.

We headed to the kitchen and started digging into the big freezer in the utility room. Cousin Will Ann kept her best jewelry in there, swearing that thieves never looked in freezers, and it was fireproof to boot. I'd tried to get her to watch The Discovery Channel, but Will Ann Lloyd knew what she knew, and documented facts weren't going to sway her.

Patricia Ann sorted through the baubles, taking the best for herself, of course, and leaving what she considered useless for her brother. She passed over some very nice costume pieces Cousin Will Ann had inherited from her mother, opting to keep the newer jewelry.

"I'm not like Mother. I can't abide anything old. New is better and more valuable," she said.

I decided not to enlighten her to the fact that older jewelry—particularly anything that had the maker's name stamped on the back—was selling for ridiculously high figures on the Internet. My husband wasn't the only member of our family who knew how to surf eBay. And Craig deserved his fair share of his mother's wealth.

We moved to the bedroom and spent a couple of hours going through Cousin Will Ann's huge wardrobe. One pile for Patricia Ann—some expensive items like furs—one pile for charity—polyester pants suits that Cousin Will Ann hadn't seemed able to part with—and a pile for throwing away—undergarments and other unmentionables. I came across a bright red teddy, extra large, mostly see-through, and managed to slip it into the toss pile before Patricia Ann saw it and started having chest pains. Why was it that adult children always reverted to the belief that they'd been brought by the stork or found in a cabbage patch?

"Let's take a break and have a glass of tea," I suggested, when the closet was empty and the last trash bag stuffed to the top. She agreed, and we stumbled over a couple of pairs of boots on our way to the kitchen.

"Having any luck?" Hank inquired from the den couch. Apparently his concern about Patricia Ann dividing up her mother's things didn't extend all the way to helping us actually do the job. No problem, but I'd certainly find a way to encourage his help in getting the stuff into Patricia Ann's car.

We moved to another room to continue the sorting job and that's when I discovered exactly what Cousin Will Ann had been up to.

CHAPTER ELEVEN

Patricia Ann took her mother's checkbook and bills folder from the desk, and plopped on the day bed in her mother's office-slash-guestroom. I knew she didn't want me to see any financial details, so I stayed in the desk chair.

"Cousin Kitty, would you mind sorting through Mother's greeting cards, recipes, photos, and the other junk she kept stashed in her desk? Feel free to take some of it home with you, unless it's something important that I should have," Patricia Ann said, tactful as always.

I nodded and reached for the long business envelopes. I was nearly out of them, so that would be a help.

My desk at home was almost exactly like Cousin Will Ann's, a smaller version of the huge old roll tops, but mine was obviously cheaper. We'd each gotten them for Christmas our freshman year in high school. For whatever reason, my mother always felt compelled to match Cousin Will Ann's mother gift for gift on every important occasion. Or top said gift when she could, which wasn't often given the differences in our parents' financial situations.

So, while my first doll was toddler-sized and wore a gingham dress, Cousin Will Ann's wore a satin bride's dress, and hers actually talked, to boot. I learned to ride on an off-brand bicycle while she pedaled around her neighborhood on a Schwinn, complete with basket and horn. My Junior Prom dress came from the Sears catalogue, Cousin Will Ann's came from an exclusive dress shop and had been the envy of every other girl at the dance. She'd spent that evening dancing with everyone else's date—leaving hers to lurk in a corner when he wasn't fetching her more punch. Somehow it had never seemed enough for her, being one up on the rest of us. She always had to shove our faces in it.

I shrugged off the old jealousy and hurt as I turned to the cubby holes. I could use the greeting cards. I was nearly out of my supply of "get wells," and I doubted Hank would be sending any to Cousin Will Ann's friends. I was fingering through "Things may look bad today," and "Your doctor said you really were a case" when I remembered something. My desk had a hidden compartment, too small to store anything bigger than a letter or two, but fun to keep Jack's love letters in when my mother was nosing around in my private stuff. Wouldn't Cousin Will Ann's desk have one as well? They were nearly identical except hers was a tad larger and made of more expensive wood.

I glanced at Patricia Ann over my shoulder. She was sucking on her thumbnail, a habit Cousin Will Ann, using hot sauce, had valiantly tried to break her from. Patricia Ann was still absorbed in her mother's bank statements and ignoring me. I reached carefully under the cubbyhole that held the long business envelopes and felt for the hinge. It was there. I slid my finger forward and tripped the latch. The molding under the cubbyholes dropped down, revealing a long flat space just large enough to hold a few business-sized folders.

I checked Patricia Ann again. Still engrossed. I slid the folders out, carefully shut the panel, and looked through them. The top folder held receipts for clothing, jewelry, and other expensive items she obviously hadn't wanted Cousin Hank to see. At least not until she was ready. The second held personal correspondence she'd received. My conscience wouldn't quite allow me to peek at those, so I moved on to the third folder. My conscience let me open that one all the way, and I barely stifled a groan. It was a report from a private investigator. The letterhead said Clete Washington, with an address over in Paducah.

Cousin Will Ann had hired a private investigator to spy on my Sunny. According to his report, Sunny had been spending time with Cousin Will Ann's son, Craig, but the private investigator hadn't seen any evidence of a romance between them beyond a peck on the cheek a few times when they'd parted. Cousin Will Ann apparently fired off a note to him to keep trying, and in response, the PI said Sunny was seeing someone else, but he didn't have the guy's ID yet. He'd get back to her soon.

"You girls want some more iced tea, or a soda?" Hank leaned against the door frame, his slightly-graying hair rumpled, eyes still swollen from lack of sleep. I nearly dropped the folders on the thick carpeting. Thankfully, my back was to him and to Patricia Ann as well.

"Yes, I'd like more iced tea," Patricia Ann said. "Cousin Kitty?"

"Ditto for me," I said, barely turning my head toward Hank.

"Be right back."

Patricia Ann stuck her nose back into the pile of bank statements, so I felt for the latch again, stuffed the folders inside the secret compartment, and shut it. I was so angry, I could've chewed the desk in half with one bite. How dare Will Ann Lloyd have my daughter followed by a private investigator? What on earth was wrong with that woman? I was finding it harder and harder to feel sorry she was gone.

Hank brought us our tea. I sipped mine and tried to calm down. One thing was certain, I'd have a talk with Cousin Will Ann's private eye and see if he'd tell me anything more, such as why she was so determined to keep Sunny and Craig apart. Was there something in Cousin Will Ann's background she was keeping secret? Was it possible that Craig and Sunny were actually related and that was why she had been trying so hard to torpedo their relationship? Or was this just one more of Cousin Will Ann's attempts to take charge of something she had no business dealing with?

And what did one wear when tackling a private investigator whom one had not hired and probably had no business questioning? Jeans and a ponytail probably wouldn't cut it.

CHAPTER TWELVE

As it turned out, I wound up wearing my exercise jerseys and a ponytail for the planned meeting with Cousin Will Ann's PI.

I left Patricia Ann still sorting through her mother's papers and drove home to fix dinner for Jack. I chose one of those box things that looked homemade when served, if the cook smiled and kept her mouth shut. We watched television until the ten o'clock news, and I went to bed. Jack opted to stay up for a late ball game.

"Kentucky's playing Vanderbilt and I don't want to miss it," he said. "I'm not really sleepy, so you go ahead."

I wondered if that was the real reason or if he was still avoiding me. I didn't have the courage to ask, yet. I knew there wasn't another woman. Even though Jack might be height challenged, he was cute as the dickens, even now, in his mid-sixties. He didn't know that, but other women saw it and when one came on to him, as a few had over the years, it made him so nervous that he'd run for cover. To me.

We'd always been open and honest with each other, which was one reason I wasn't pressing him now with questions. Also, to be honest, I wasn't sure I'd like the answers. This "avoidance" had been going on since before Cousin Will Ann died, so I knew her murder hadn't caused his problem. If it wasn't another woman, then maybe he'd simply grown tired of me. Something I'd never thought could happen given the intensity of his feelings over the years and how he'd expressed them physically, if not in words.

Or maybe he was ill. I chewed my lip and thought that over. He did have that appointment with the surgeon, the appointment he hadn't bothered to tell me about. That possibility worried me the most. We'd been together most of our lives. I couldn't imagine living without him. I finally fell asleep, still mulling the possibilities.

I awoke the next morning to find Jack gone again. I slid into my jerseys, pulled my hair back, tracked him down in the garage, kissed him good-bye, and headed to aerobics. He was still working on the shelves in the garage when I backed out. I was grateful for that. Our Christmas decorations had swelled to proportions that likely rivaled those of the White House, and storing them became more challenging by the year.

Debby met me at the door of the Senior Center. "How'd it go at Will Ann's house yesterday?"

"Fine," I hedged.

She squinted at me suspiciously. The major problem with best friends was that they could spot an issue-duck a mile away. I busied myself warming up. Thankfully, I'd arrived a bit late and Shirley Mumfort fired up her CD player and clapped for our attention before Debby could quiz me further. For the next thirty minutes Shirley tortured us with moves that would have crippled less determined women.

"I'm grateful we aren't actually paying Shirley to abuse us like this," Debby whispered during a break. I nodded and guzzled my water. Before we'd become eligible to use the Senior Center, our group had paid to exercise. Looking back, I did have to wonder at our intelligence, or lack thereof, back then.

"You sure you're okay?" she prodded.

"I'm fine. It was just difficult, going through Cousin Will Ann's things. We leave so much behind when we die. Makes you wonder why we bother to collect it all in the first place, just for someone else to enjoy." I walked to the small refrigerator in the corner and pulled out one of the cold towels Shirley stored there, wrapping it around my neck. Shirley might be tougher than a frustrated drill sergeant, but she knew how to take care of her troops.

"I know," Debby called after me. "I sometimes get that same feeling when I walk into an antique store. All those beautiful things going to strangers."

"Yeah, but you keep going there," I argued.

"Sure, because I give those things the tender loving care they deserve. And I enjoy them." She mopped her face with her towel.

Shirley was unrolling her workout mat for the yoga cooldown. I reached for my mat. "But what about when it's your stuff in that store someday?"

"I'll be gone by then," Debby reasoned, "so I won't know about it, and I would hope whomever buys my things will enjoy them as much as I have. Stop being so morbid. Besides, you know Will Ann would have a stroke at the thought of anyone else touching her things. That alone should've made it a worthwhile job for you."

I was saved having to answer her when Shirley flopped onto the mat and curled herself into a position I wasn't at all sure I could match. Even as a child, I'd never been able to do the splits. Long legs but short hamstring muscles. Simple leg stretches were a challenge for me. I dropped gracelessly onto the mat and gave it a shot. Debby was already pulling her leg behind her hip in a way that had to hurt.

After class I declined my usual luncheon with the girls, stating I had errands to run in Paducah. They didn't bother to question me because Paducah was the nearest large city to us, boasting not only a mall but two—count 'em—Wal-Marts. We Metropolis folks did a lot of our business across the river.

Since I wasn't quite as sweaty as usual, I decided to go as I was. If I went back home for a shower, Jack might ask questions about where I was going. I never lied to him. Okay, maybe I didn't quite share every single thing I ever knew, but I did not lie, and I wasn't about to start now. I'd just head over to Paducah, keep the appointment I'd made for this afternoon with the private investigator Cousin Will Ann had hired to follow my daughter, and see if I could ferret out what he knew.

The sorrow I'd felt at Cousin Will Ann's death had once again been replaced by anger. What had been wrong with the woman? Sunny was beautiful, intelligent, warm and caring. Any man would be lucky to have her. If Cousin Will Ann hadn't seen that, then she'd needed new glasses. Or, as Debby had suggested, a smack upside the head.

I decided to skip the I-24 bridge and drive to Paducah via the old Brookport Bridge on Highway 45. It would take me across the Ohio River and straight toward the old part of town where many of the abandoned buildings were being renovated into homes and businesses. Clete Washington had his office there, on Eighth Street. Since he wasn't in a fancier, more expensive neighborhood, I had high hopes that the offer of money would be all the incentive he'd need to tell me what I wanted to know.

I gritted my teeth and shot up onto the old blue bridge, fingers firmly gripping the steering wheel. The metal decking always made Beetle do a jitter bug, and the narrow width gave the impression that I was about to be sideswiped by cars going in the opposite direction. Meeting a semi on the bridge, even in a Volkswagen, was a nightmare. No semis were in sight, nor were many other vehicles, so I relaxed and bounced across the long span and enjoyed my latest Yanni tape. Peeking down at the river, I noticed it was white-capping. As long as the rain held off in those dark swirling clouds overhead, I'd be fine.

I glanced in the rear-view mirror as a red van zoomed up behind me. It looked like Maggie's, and the driver might have taken lessons from her, judging from the nearness of the van's front to my rear bumper. If it turned out to be Maggie, she'd soon get a lecture the likes of which she hadn't heard since high school when she'd backed Jack's truck into a tree.

I sped up a bit over the twenty-five-mile-per-hour limit on the bridge and checked the mirrors every few seconds, but the van stayed on my tail. I couldn't see the driver through the tinted window. If it was Maggie, and if she had my grandchildren with her, I swore I'd give her a spanking right in front of them. She should not be driving like that just to tease me, if her children were in the van. Not to mention putting her mother in harm's way.

The whine of my tires on the metal decking increased as I crossed the last of the straight section and started the downhill descent. The van edged closer. I gripped the wheel tighter. Was the driver going to pass me on the bridge, even though the entire span was a "no passing" zone? People were known to pass on the bridge, even though it was extremely dangerous to do so. Usually it was kids with no fear and less sense. But I really couldn't picture a teenager driving a red "mommy van." Not willingly.

Beetle and the red van reached the end of the span and zipped past the guard rails. I assumed the driver would pass me now that it was a bit safer to do so. There was barely enough room for the breeze to blow between our bumpers.

The van rammed my rear bumper, causing me to swing wide to the right. I frantically spun the wheel, trying to correct my direction, but it was too late. Beetle shot over the shoulder and dived forward over the hill, bouncing and rolling end over end like a black roly-poly bug until I thought my guts would fall out. We finally shuddered to a stop in the thick stand of trees and bushes below the highway.

CHAPTER THIRTEEN

I awoke with the sunlight knifing into my eyes as it bounced off the rearview mirror. I moved the mirror and pulled down the visor. Wait! What was I doing napping inside my bug? I glanced around and took a deep breath, as deep as the steering wheel would allow. Breathing hurt. Not a good sign.

Beetle was crushed around me like a used soda can. The roof was way too low for my comfort, and the back seat was now part of the front. There didn't seem to be a passenger side any more.

I often felt claustrophobic in small enclosed areas. Even though Beetle was a little car, driving it hadn't bothered me because it had big windows. But having it wrapped around me as tightly as a newborn baby in a receiving blanket was not my idea of cozy. I had to get out of there.

I tried to move my legs, and discovered that one of them was broken. I couldn't see or feel the other one. I hoped it was still there somewhere under the dash. The stick shift had been shoved between the seats, and I couldn't even see the knob on top of it. I wiped the blood out of my eyes. Why did head cuts always bleed like a major artery had been severed?

I listened for the sound of someone rushing to my aide. No sirens, so help hadn't arrived on the scene yet. But they'd surely be here soon. How long had I been in this mess? And how had I gotten here?

Somehow, I managed to untangle my left arm from the steering wheel and check my watch. One o'clock. Jack and I usually had lunch at twelve, except for the days when I had aerobics. So what was I doing here in my wrecked bug? Had I been on my way home from a restaurant when this happened? Did I have an appointment somewhere? An appointment that I was about to be very late for?

And where, exactly, was here? My back was jammed against the driver's door, so I couldn't see out that way. I looked through what was left of the windshield. Dense foliage covered Beetle's entire front trunk area, and leaves poked through the broken glass near the passenger side door. I couldn't see much out of that window, either, since the trunk lid was plastered against it. I tilted the rear view mirror again, but there was nothing but greenery behind me.

I must be in a wooded area. Which could be anywhere around Metropolis. Or Brookport. I tried to think about what I'd been doing or where I'd been going. I had on my exercise jerseys, so I must have been to aerobics. But what day was it? Had I been to church last night? That was how I usually kept the days straight, by when I'd last been to church. I couldn't even remember.

Having seen the damage to the windshield and roof, I was thankful I always wore a seatbelt. But my heart ached with the knowledge that Beetle was finished. We'd ridden together a long time.

My head hurt like crazy. Ditto for my leg and just about every other part of my body. Thankfully, my purse was still beside me, the strap hooked under my seatbelt. I dug into the depths of the purse and came out with a couple of aspirins from one pocket, and the small water bottle I usually carried in a baggie stuffed into another. Might as well relax until help arrived.

When I woke again, it was dark and I was still trapped inside

Beetle. My head had stopped hurting and the blood had dried. By now my leg was numb. I still didn't know if that was good or bad. I pressed the little button on my watch. Seven thirty. Six and a half hours since the accident, if not longer. And no one had come to rescue me. Surely someone had seen it happen.

Where was Jack? Where were our girls? Had no one missed me? I tried to think back, but still couldn't remember where I'd been going before I wound up in this mess.

I listened again. I could hear frogs singing, so I must be near water, unless they were tree frogs. By sight I could tell a tree frog from, say, a leopard-spotted frog, but not by song. I should've paid more attention in college biology.

Above and behind me, I heard the whoosh of a passing car. So I was somewhere near a road. But not a heavily traveled one. Must've run off it somehow. Jack always said I drove too close to the shoulder. Easy for Jack to say. He generally took his half out of the middle, often courting disaster from a head-on collision.

Several minutes went by before I heard another vehicle. This one lumbered above me. It made a brapping sound as the driver downshifted. Must be a tractor trailer. Which meant I was close to a highway, but one that was not heavily used at night. Probably Highway 45. Which also meant someone should have seen me by now. And hadn't. I had to get help, but how?

I'd heard stories on the news about cars going off steep embankments, not to be found for days, even weeks, and usually with the driver dead by the time help arrived. I remembered one local case in particular where a wrecked vehicle hadn't been spotted until late the next winter, when all the leaves fell off the trees. The driver had gone off the shoulder on the Kentucky side of the Brookport Bridge. Could that be where I was? And all that time the poor woman's family hadn't known what'd happened to her. She'd simply been listed as a missing person.

I didn't want that to happen to my family. Jack must be getting frantic. He'd probably already called Debby or some of the girls at aerobics, to see when I'd left. Since undoubtedly no one had seen me since one o'clock, he'd surely be out searching for me by now.

What if I'd been on my way somewhere, and he wasn't expecting me home for several hours? But I never traveled alone at night. I either went with him or a friend. Too dangerous for a woman at night by herself, even in a small town like Metropolis. Or a larger one like Paducah.

I checked my watch again. Only seven thirty-five now. I was hungry. Assuming I'd had lunch, it had worn off. Well, former Girl Scouts are just as prepared as their male counterparts. I dug in my bag and came out with a snack bar. I knew I had at least two in there, but still, I'd have to ration myself. Just in case.

Another vehicle swooshed by. I yelled for help. Then I laughed at myself. That hurt as well. Yes, it was warm weather, but how many people drove with their windows down? Most had the air conditioner on and the windows rolled up tight. And young people who did have the windows down had their music cranked up high, willing to share the sounds with anyone within a five block distance.

I waited several minutes until I heard another car and tried honking Beetle's horn. No one stopped. I reached for the headlight switch, but nothing happened. Beetle's front end must have sustained too much damage. Terrific. At least if the lights had worked, I could've left them on as a beacon. For as long as the battery held its charge, anyhow.

Now what?

I leaned back against the window and rested my head. The

pain around my ribs was still pretty bad, and I could only take shallow breaths. Mosquitoes buzzed my ears, taking a few bites out of my cheeks now and then, making me wonder for the millionth time why Noah hadn't had enough brains to leave them off his ark. My other leg had grown numb, which was a blessing for the moment, but I did have to wonder if I'd ever walk again.

Assuming I managed to get out of this mess.

I wished Jack was here. Not involved in the accident, of course, just here to comfort me until someone arrived to pry me out and take me to the hospital. First I'd kiss him, and then I'd brain him for refusing to let us get a cell phone when I'd begged for one.

His grandmother hadn't needed one, he said, and she'd traveled the local highways and crossed the bridges many-a-time with no problem. Ditto for his mother. Well, neither one of them ever lay trapped for hours in a crushed vehicle with no help in sight.

If I did get out of this mess, I'd have me a cell phone, and maybe even insist we buy a car with that new-fangled technology I'd seen on TV where they knew the minute you had a wreck and where you were when you had it. And they sent help. Quickly.

Technology, schmechnology, Jack Bloodworth was going to have to learn to live with it or live without me.

Assuming, of course, I didn't kill him first.

CHAPTER FOURTEEN

"Kitty!"

Jack was calling my name. I tried to pull the pillow over my head, but I couldn't find it.

"Kitty, can you hear me? Kitty, please answer me."

Oh, dear. He sounded really upset. Scheherazade must've had her kittens in the back seat of the Chevy again, leaving her usual post-natal mess behind.

Jack always threatened to drop her at the humane society when she did that, but it was his own fault for leaving the car window down, even a crack. She was as supple as a mouse and just as able to squeeze into places where she didn't belong, even when ready to drop a litter. Of course he'd blame me for not having her fixed. I kept promising to do that, but every time I got ready, she was already pregnant again. Such a slut.

I'd give him a few minutes to calm down. When my eyes opened all the way, I'd go out there to the garage and offer to wipe off the seats for him.

I started to turn over and every single part of my body hurt, particularly my head. And Jack's shouting certainly wasn't helping. I opened my eyes, peeked around, and realized I was not at home in bed. I was surrounded by crushed glass and metal. Was this some sort of nightmare? I was prone to them, particularly since I'd started the new allergy medicine.

Jack seemed to be pounding on something behind my head. I turned and saw his face. Something was wrong. Bad wrong.

And this was no nightmare.

I tried to move, but he shouted at me to lie still. He said he was going for help.

Go where? Get what kind of help?

I watched as he disappeared through the greenery that surrounded me, but the crick in my neck made it impossible to keep looking. I turned and surveyed my surroundings. My head felt funny, as though there was a large clock inside pounding out the seconds. My contact lenses were so foggy I could barely see. I wondered where my bedside drops were. I ran a hand across my forehead and discovered it was hot enough to fry an egg on. No wonder everything seemed strange. I must have the flu. Which meant I'd blown seven bucks for nothing for the flu-shot my doctor insisted on giving me. I'd have a word or two with him about that.

I heard a thump and looked around. Jack was back, shouting something about help on the way and for me to hang on.

Hang on to what? I was sick, not dangling from a precipice. Did he have a fever as well? It wouldn't have surprised me. He always had to be sick whenever I was, only his illness was always worse and required far more care.

"Get me a drink," I croaked.

"Hang on. I've got a bottle in the truck." He moved a step and came back. "Kitty Bloodworth, don't you dare die and leave me."

I attempted a nod, but the pain was too great. He was back in a short time, but he couldn't seem to figure out a way to get the bottle to me through the glass separating us. He crawled around to the other side and passed me the bottle through an opening.

What was this place, anyhow? And how had I gotten here? It still felt like a nightmare, but the pain let me know it was real.

"I'm so thankful I found you!" he shouted. "We've been looking all night."

All night? Where had I been all night? And where in the world was I now? I tried to ask, but the words wouldn't come out.

I heard Jack shouting, "Down here! We're down here, please, hurry!"

Well, at least I knew what direction I was in. Down.

A Paducah police officer stood beside Jack. The police officer breathed heavily. Wherever "down" was, it must be a difficult trip. I sincerely hoped they didn't expect me to walk back to wherever "up" was, because I certainly wasn't able to do it. And Jack couldn't carry me.

I'd always been a bit taller than he, and carrying me over the threshold on our wedding night hadn't been a pretty sight. I would've laughed now, but it would hurt too much. Mercy, it felt like I'd been run over by a truck. And maybe the driver had backed up to make sure he hadn't missed me. What else could hurt this bad?

Another head popped up near the window, this one with a navy EMT jacket underneath. "Rescue team is on their way," he said. "They'll need the jaws of life to get her out. Any idea how long she's been in there?" He swatted at a fly, then pointed in my direction.

Sure, talk about me like I'm not even here, young man. Wait until I got over this flu bug. We'd have a chat.

Once I figured out what was going on.

"Kitty, honey, stay calm," Jack said. "We'll have you out of there in a few minutes."

Out of where? Had I fallen into our old well? No, couldn't be, or I'd be surrounded by water. What was all this metal and glass?

I heard thrashing sounds, and a fireman appeared, carrying equipment. "Any gas leaks?" he asked.

"I don't smell any," Jack said. "Please, get her out of there.

She's been trapped in the wreckage since yesterday."

Yesterday? That couldn't be, because yesterday I'd been . . .

Where exactly had I been yesterday? I tried to think, but even thinking made me hurt. All over.

I heard more voices, then the sound of some sort of engine firing up. Whatever I was lying on began to shake, and the noises were deafening. I closed my eyes and prayed.

CHAPTER FIFTEEN

I awoke in what I assumed was the emergency room. We'd been there often enough with the girls when they were little.

Was that why I was here now? Was one of the girls hurt or sick?

No, that couldn't be, since I was the one on the bed. I could hear Jack just outside the curtain around my bed. He was talking to someone in a loud whisper. I caught snatches of "Serious, possibly life-threatening" and "Must stay calm, not upset her."

Upset who? Me? I was too ill to be upset, and I hurt too much. I'd never had a flu like this flu. It felt like every bone in my body was broken. Just breathing was a major effort.

I heard the curtain scrape aside and opened my eyes to see Jack step inside, followed by Sunny and Maggie. I hoped Maggie had the good sense, for once, not to bring the kids. I sure didn't want them to catch this flu.

"Where are the kids?" I whispered.

"Debby's outside with them, in the waiting room. She rushed here as soon as Dad called. Joe's on his way."

"Send them all home. Don't want the kids catching this."

"Catching what?" Maggie asked.

Sunny started toward me, looking for all the world like she was going to throw herself on the bed with me. I cringed, but thankfully Jack caught her in time.

"Don't touch Mom until we see what the doctor says," Jack

cautioned. "He's taking X-rays in a few minutes. Maybe even an MRI."

MRI? For the flu? No doubt about it, Jack Bloodworth was losing it. I'd been worrying about his short term memory loss lately, and now I had proof.

"Oh, Mom," Maggie moaned. "You look awful!"

Gee, thanks, just what every mother wants to hear. And how would she feel with a body temperature that couldn't be much lower than a hundred and twenty degrees, judging by how my head was pounding? In fact, my whole body hurt, and I could barely breathe.

Maggie must've read my look, because she started to cry. I never could stand it when my babies cried, even one who had babies of her own. I managed to squeeze the hand she'd stroked my arm with.

"I'll be fine," I whispered.

I hoped I was telling the truth. I suspected right now death would be the easy way out. During the MRI I managed to nap, or faint, or whatever it was I kept doing whenever the pain became too much. The MRI is not a good test for someone who is claustrophobic, for someone who knocks people out of the way in order to exit an elevator—whenever her husband manages to drag her onto one.

I'd just settled back into place in the emergency room when Dr. Twining entered my cubicle to deliver the good news. I'd had him as a student in fourth grade, when I subbed for his teacher who was out on maternity leave. I'd privately suspected she'd had a baby on purpose, in order to avoid finishing out the year with young Master Twining. His attitude of knowing more than the teacher—not to mention correcting her whenever he suspected she'd made an error—had not endeared him to her, or anyone else on the faculty.

"Compound fractures of the left leg. We'll have to set the

breaks in surgery."

Surgery?

"Surgery?" Jack said.

"Probably have to use some pins. She'll be in a cast for quite some time."

Terrific. A broken leg. What could top that? And how had I managed to break it? A fall down the basement stairs?

"Couple of cracked ribs," Dr. Twining continued. "We'll tape them lightly. Mostly they just have to heal on their own. We will have to re-inflate that lung, of course."

Re-inflate? Oh, that sounded like fun. And . . . ?

"The head injury isn't too serious, minor concussion, probably kept her knocked out through the worst of it."

Lot you know, you little twerp.

"Our major concern right now, of course, is the collapsed lung. She's running a pretty high fever. Infection's probably already set in."

No kidding. What gave you your first clue? My sky-high temp or the wheezy breathing?

"We'll have to keep a close eye on that lung, to make sure she doesn't develop full-blown pneumonia. That could be fatal in someone her age. But the antibiotics will help. Just remember, no singing or loud talking for a few days." He winked at me through his thick glasses.

Like I was in any shape to sing or shout?

"We'll re-inflate the lung first, in a few minutes, then set the leg."

Do tell. Any more good news?

"And she'll need extensive therapy both before and after she goes home. We'll have to keep her here for several days. Injuries like this are often fatal to the elderly."

And with that, the male version of Little Mary Sunshine departed. I presumed he wanted to set the wheels in motion to torture me further.

Elderly, schmelderly. But could Twining be right? Was I in danger?

"Oh, Mommy, I'm so sorry," Maggie said. "This is all my fault."

Her fault?

CHAPTER SIXTEEN

"Would someone just fill me in," I croaked again, "about how I got here? What happened? How did I manage to break a leg and collapse a lung?"

Frankly, I never knew breathing could hurt this much.

"The doctor said you need to rest, Mom," Sunny said. "We can fill you in later." She glared at her sister.

I made a rude comment about the doctor and where he should wear his stethoscope in the future, but I managed to deliver it without swearing or shouting. Maggie giggled and Sunny looked shocked.

"I simply meant I'd like to strangle him with it," I said. "What did you think I meant? Now, give me some answers."

Jack, Maggie and Sunny exchanged glances. Maggie started crying again and Sunny put her arms around her sister's shoulders. That left Jack. He cleared his throat and gave it a shot.

"When you didn't come home for lunch yesterday, I wasn't too worried." He reached down and stroked my fingers. "Figured you'd had lunch with the girls after aerobics."

That sounded sensible. But yesterday? What time was it now?

"You still weren't home by late afternoon, so I assumed you and Debby were shopping. When you didn't show up for supper, I got worried. I called Debby, but she hadn't seen you since aerobics. You'd told her you had an important errand over in Paducah and you were skipping lunch. You didn't tell her what the errand was."

He looked expectantly at me. I shook my head and whispered, "I have no idea where I was going. Don't even remember going to aerobics."

I knew I must have gone there, though. The nurse in the ER had cut my favorite jerseys to shreds getting them off me. Not that I minded. They were covered in blood. Now I was generously attired in one of those thin, open-backed hospital gowns that reduced all patients to the level of pre-kindergarteners.

"I called all of your friends," Jack continued, "but no one knew where you were. Maggie said she'd come over and help me look for you. That's when she discovered her van was missing."

I turned my head carefully to look at Maggie, still sobbing in her sister's arms. Was it for me or the van? Possibly a toss-up.

"Where was I, and how did you find me?" I managed.

"We drove around for hours, both in Metropolis and in Paducah, looking for you. We searched all along the I-24 bridge, in case you went off into one of the fields." Jack stopped to wipe a tear.

I'd seen that man cry a grand total of two times in forty-plus years, and that was on the day each of our daughters were born. Not a tear when our baby son was born dead, or when Jack's parents died, or mine, because he thought he had to be strong for the rest of us. And when our grandbabies had come along, he'd laughed for joy.

This must be pretty bad. I reached for his hand.

"The Metropolis and Paducah police helped us, Mom," Sunny said. "But we couldn't find a trace of you or your bug anywhere."

"You should have told me where you were going," Jack said.

Sunny pounced. "And you should have bought her a cell phone when she asked for one, Daddy. Then she could have called for help right away. Mother could have died down in that gulley before you found her."

Jack hung his head. I squeezed his hand again, even though the effort was painful. "It wasn't your fault, honey. I should have told you. I don't know why I didn't, and right now I have no idea where I was going."

"The doctor told us you might have trouble with your memory for a while. He said the accident might come back to you, and it might not. We'll just have to wait and see."

More good news. Did the charming Doctor Twining never run out of negative things to say about his patients?

"What about the gulley?" I asked.

Jack held the straw, giving me a sip of water, and ordered me to stop asking questions.

"Then give me the answers, please."

"I was fairly certain you'd had an accident," he said. "Couldn't let myself think you'd been kidnapped or anything."

Another tear-swipe. "We'd searched everywhere else," he continued, "so this morning I took a chance and drove over the Brookport Bridge, even though I know you rarely go that way. I spotted a van that looked like Maggie's, so I checked it out. It was parked next to the dumpster behind the gas station just beyond the bridge. When I looked through a back window I knew it was hers because Billy's pink bunny was in his seat. And I could see that her van had been in an accident."

He looked at me as if to gauge how I was taking this information. "I figured you had to be involved somehow, so I started checking the area. I remembered the news story about someone being found down below the bridge months after a wreck, still inside the vehicle." He swallowed hard. "Dead."

The rest of his words came out in a series of sobs. "I drove back toward the bridge and spotted some gouges in the hillside above those bushes. I turned around, parked, and hiked down.

That's when I found you. I thought you were gone."

I started to cry with him. That must have been tough.

"If you'd had a cell phone, Daddy, you could have dialed 9-1-1 instead of risking life and limb waving down a truck on the bridge. What if that guy had hit you? Who would have known—"

"Young lady," I gasped, interrupting Sunny's tirade. "Enough about cell phones, and you aren't too old for a smack on the rear end—just as soon as I get well enough—if I hear you speak to your father that way again."

That response took all the energy I had. I shut my eyes and thought over what Jack had said. Maggie's van stolen? By whom? And why was it wrecked and parked not far from where I was found. If she wasn't driving it, and I certainly wasn't, then who was?

I felt Maggie touch my hair, probably the only part of me that didn't hurt. "Mom, I'm so sorry. This is all my fault. I'd been to the grocery, and when I got home, the kids were fighting, and I was trying to grab them and the grocery bags and . . ." she paused, "I left my keys in the ignition."

I opened one eye and glared at her.

"I know, you've warned me about that dozens of times. I just never thought anyone would steal my van in our quiet little neighborhood. And now you're hurt, and the van is wrecked, and Joe is threatening to kill me, and . . ." She went to pieces again.

Sunny said, "You know, Mom, I've been thinking. Like Dad said, you never use the Brookport Bridge. You always drive over to Paducah on I-24."

She turned to her dad.

"Maybe Mom saw someone driving Maggie's van, someone who shouldn't have been behind the wheel. Maggie, what time did you get home from the grocery store?"

"About eleven. Maybe a little after." Maggie snuffled.

"Just about the time Mom would've been leaving aerobics. She could've easily spotted the van and decided to follow it. It's just like something you would do, Mom. And without a cell—"

"Sunny!"

"Okay, Mom, but that could explain why Maggie's van was found just a few hundred yards from where you were. Like Dad said, whoever abandoned it left it right near the Smoke Shop, just below the bridge. You were close to the bridge, on the other side of the road. It all fits."

Yes, it did all fit. We'd probably never know who swiped Maggie's van. Or how I came to run off the road chasing after it. That had to be one of the dumbest things I'd ever done. I grinned until my cheeks stung and wondered why my face itched like crazy.

"What's so funny, Mom?" Maggie asked.

"I was just thinking, Cousin Will Ann will really ride me hard over this one. I hate it whenever I hand her enough ammunition to shoot me down with."

My daughters and my husband looked at each other, then at me, mouths swinging open.

I said, "What?"

Jack took my hand again. "Honey, Will Ann's dead. Don't you remember?"

Of course I didn't remember. Did he think I'd forget something that important?

"If this is a joke, it isn't funny," I whispered.

Maggie sat on the end of the bed, careful not to touch me.

"Mom, it isn't a joke. Cousin Will Ann is dead. We buried her several days ago. You helped serve at the gathering afterwards. Don't you remember any of that?

I closed my eyes and pictured Cousin Will Ann, but I couldn't come up with a vision of her in a casket. Certainly not one of her being forever silent. Will Ann Lloyd always out-talked anyone in the room, except possibly me, only what she said was always tinged with sarcasm that cut to the quick.

Dead? I hadn't thought anything could ever kill her. I shivered, and I knew it wasn't just from lying in a cold cubicle in the emergency room. How could I not remember being at her funeral? How could I not remember being in a serious accident? Was Dr. Twerp right about my memory? Would it ever come back?

The doctor in question re-entered my cubicle with a nurse who carried a tray full of equipment, none of which I wanted touching my body.

My daughters, the cowards, fled. Jack held my hand for what was probably the longest few minutes of my life. After a localized shot for pain, a chest tube was inserted to drain the air that didn't belong around the outside of my lung. As soon as the lung re-expanded, the pain level dropped and breathing became easier. I could've kissed Dr. Twerp. Almost.

Instead, I kissed Jack goodbye as they wheeled me toward surgery to set my broken bones.

CHAPTER SEVENTEEN

Resting somewhat more comfortably late the next morning in my private hospital room, I still couldn't believe it. Cousin Will Ann dead. And what was worse, I couldn't remember finding her body, probably a good thing, or the funeral, not a good thing. I should at least be able to remember paying my respects. Jack and the girls had told me about Detective Parker and the fact that our family members were at the top of his list of suspects.

Naturally, I wasn't thrilled to hear the part about Cousin Will Ann storming into Farley's Cafeteria, calling Sunny names, and flouncing back out. That was Will Ann's usual modus operandi, hit-and-run. I was thankful to know we all had solid alibis, but I wished I could've remembered those past few days.

"They don't have any idea who killed her?" I asked the group surrounding my bed.

Jack sat nearby, holding my hand. Sunny perched on the large windowsill, and Maggie and Joe shared the large chair at the foot of the bed. They exchanged glances again. I was beginning to hate that look. I was almost thankful my grandchildren were with Joe's mom, knowing I couldn't handle a hundred hugs, kisses and questions on this particular morning.

"Parker suspects every single person in Cousin Will Ann's family, including us," Joe said as Maggie nudged him in the ribs.

"Yes," Sunny jumped in, "but all of us can account for our

time that night. You and Dad were with the car club at Farley's. Craig and I were studying together. Patricia Ann was on television. Maggie, Joe, and the kids were at a chili supper. And Cousin Hank was at a chamber meeting."

I nodded. That was certainly welcome news. "Hand me the cortisone crème, Sunny, please. My face itches like crazy. The nurse said it was mosquito bites, another plus from the accident."

She opened the tube and squeezed the crème into my palm. I rubbed some on and felt instant relief. Too bad I hadn't known about this wonderful stuff when I'd been a kid playing in the woods around my parents' home.

"But how did anyone manage to put her in our trunk?" I asked. "Cousin Will Ann wasn't exactly teensy."

"That's what puzzles me," Maggie said. "Apparently, you saw her BMW pulling away from Farley's, Mother. The next time anyone saw her, she was in Sadie's trunk."

"Didn't Cousin Hank miss her that night? Particularly when he got home from the meeting and she wasn't there?" I asked.

"She told him she was spending the night in Paducah with Patricia Ann because she had business there early the next morning. But Patricia Ann swears Cousin Will Ann never said any such thing to her."

I worried that over for a few minutes. At least we were all in the clear. But it seemed mighty convenient to me that Cousin Will Ann wound up in Sadie's trunk just before an important competition, and I was determined to figure out who had stuffed her in there.

My to-do list had only one item on it at the moment: survive. When my lung healed and I got through enough therapy to go home, I might be able to pull on my thinking cap and come up with some answers. Unless it had been a random killing. But that couldn't be. They'd have left Cousin Will Ann wherever they killed her, if that were the case. No, this had to be someone we knew, someone who knew our habits, knew how to get into our pole barn, and when it would be safe to hide Will Ann's body there.

Could the theft of Maggie's van be somehow related to Cousin Will Ann's murder? I didn't see how. But the mother part of me that knew when things were important wouldn't let me ignore it. When I was able, I'd shake the extended family tree and see who fell out. Just as long as it wasn't someone on a branch close to mine.

I knew that, eventually, I'd have a good cry over Cousin Will Ann's murder, and I'd probably remember only the good times we'd had and forget the bad, but for right now I stored all the information my family had given me in the back of my mind, to take out later.

Joe stood and reached for Maggie's hand. "We'd better go rescue my mom. The kids made her promise to let them help bake cookies. According to my watch, the fire department should be arriving at her house just about now." He moved to the bed, leaned over and gently kissed my forehead. "Of course, nothing like that ever happens when they stay at your house, does it?" He flashed a large-toothed grin at me and stepped aside for Maggie's goodbye kiss.

"Well, there was that time when we had to call in the Navy SEALS," I said. "But older toilets do have their problems."

Joe laughed, but Maggie looked as though she was actually buying my poor attempt at humor as she followed him to the door.

"I've got to run as well, Mom. Craig needs help with a term paper," Sunny said. "And please don't worry yourself over Cousin Will Ann's murder. Right now you need to concentrate on getting well." With that, she kissed my other cheek and left.

Jack reached for the phone book on the table beside my bed.

"Want me to order in some pizza? It's bound to beat whatever the hospital is serving for lunch."

"Make it thin crust," I said. Jack wasn't overly fond of pizza—particularly thick crust, which I loved—so he was either cheering me up or changing the subject to get my mind off Cousin Will Ann.

As I listened to him place the order, I snuggled under the quilt Jack had brought from our house to keep me warm and wondered if my short-term memory would ever return. Particularly the part about me chasing Maggie's car thief and how I'd wound up in the bushes several hundred yards downhill from the highway. If a person was going to make a total fool out of herself, it seemed to me she ought to at least be able to remember doing it.

CHAPTER EIGHTEEN

A few days later I was trying to find a more comfortable position on the narrow hospital bed for my good leg when Dr. Twerp stuck his head in the doorway. I sincerely hoped he only intended to charge me half price for his hospital visits since I'd rarely seen more than half of his body poking through my door. Heaven forbid he should actually approach the bed and check my pulse. Who knew how much such in-depth medical care would cost me?

"We're starting you on physical therapy tomorrow, Kitty. This is Russ, and he'll be in charge of you."

A youngish version of Hulk Hogan leaned over Dr. Twerp's shoulder and waved. Great. Let the pain begin.

"The antibiotics are taking care of the pneumonia," Twerp said. "So it's time to get you out of that bed. Of course, it's up to you whether or not you walk again because women of your age usually don't have what it takes to overcome this kind of challenge."

I gritted my teeth until my jaw ached and nodded at Russ. Challenge, schmallenge. I'd soon be on my feet again, even if it killed me. Then I'd kill Dr. Twerp. It would be worth spending the rest of my life in prison.

"Thank you, Doctor. I'm sure Russ and I will work well together."

They left me pouting and plotting painful ways to accomplish Twerp's demise. Walking would obviously be painful for a very long time, but I would walk again. And laugh, and love. Maybe I'd even be able to run in the annual Superman 4K next year. I'd taken third place in my age division this year. The fact that there were only two other women in my age group and that all I had to do to take third place was cross the finish line upright and mobile hadn't fazed me one bit. I'd done that, albeit in dead last position, but I'd won a plaque. I am woman, hear me wheeze.

"Kitty, it's so good to see you still breathing!" Wendy Sikes swooped down on my hospital bed with an enveloping hug and an arm full of flowers. I was afraid for a minute she'd smother me.

Jack was out hunting us a decent lunch, Debby had already been by for her daily visit, and the girls weren't coming until after supper, so I was trapped.

"Lilies," I said. "How thoughtful." Truth be told, they reminded me of my mother's funeral.

"I said to Harry I was sure you'd be riding in his hearse instead of Jack's old Chevy the next time we saw you," she said, tongue engaged, brain obviously not in gear. "He said I was crazy. Nothing could keep you down." I watched her henna curls bounce as she talked. Wendy certainly wasn't the sharpest knife in the drawer.

I forced a smile. "You tell Harry I'd dearly love a ride in that vintage hearse of his. But only if I can sit up front while he leads the rest of the Super Cruisers down Market Street for the Christmas parade."

"It's a shame our old church building isn't handicap accessible in the downstairs area," she said, switching subjects with the speed of light. "I'm surprised the city of Metropolis hasn't made us upgrade it." She dumped the flowers on my lap then put a white-gloved hand to her lips. "Not that we'd want them crossing the line between separation of church and state with us, of course."

"I almost wish they would," I said, easing the huge bouquet off my bad leg. "It will be a mighty long time before I can maneuver down those narrow stairs to teach my class."

I reached for the call button in hopes of summoning a nurse to relieve me of the flowers. "Once I'm well enough to attend church, I'll have to sit in on the auditorium class. I simply cannot believe Baylor Tidwell is still teaching the history of the church. It didn't take that long for our ancestors to live it!"

Wendy snickered in agreement and promised she and Harry would buy Jack's and my lunch as soon as I was able to get out and about to attend church. I quickly accepted. Like I said, my momma hadn't raised any dummies.

Wendy dusted pollen off her navy skirt and scooted her chair closer to the hospital bed. "I know it's awful, but things seem much less stressful at church with your cousin Will Ann gone."

She glanced at the open door, turned back to me, and in a stage whisper said, "That woman put me under a microscope when her children were in my class years ago, and even after they moved into the adult class she still stuck her nose in the door at least once a quarter to see if my classroom was decorated in the proper manner and whether or not I was using the books the elders purchased." Another snort. "Like I haven't been doing all of that practically since she was in the third grade."

I nodded. "She treated all the teachers that way."

"I know, but that's not the worst of it. She always refused to teach a class herself even when her kids were little and our congregation was much smaller. And she certainly never helped us out when it was time to file things in the resource room."

I struggled to keep my mouth shut, not wishing to speak ill of the dead, even if the dead was my cousin and deserved it.

"I hate to say it, but she was an awful gossip," Wendy

continued. "Of course, that's exactly what I'm doing right now, gossiping about her, and she isn't here to defend herself, but I wouldn't have had the courage when she was still alive. She was a real terror if she set her bead on you. I mostly tried to stay out of her sight line."

Wendy straightened her pill box hat and glanced at the door again, as if she thought the gossip police were about to pounce. "But I think you should know that before she was killed she came looking for you one Wednesday night right after class. And she was strongly hinting that there was trouble between you and Jack."

Say what?

"What kind of trouble between Jack and me? We're fine, always have been," I said.

At least for all the time I could remember. And I was only missing the few days between a Wal-Mart run with Maggie and waking up in the hospital. Surely we couldn't have had any serious marital trouble in that short amount of time, could we? Was my memory missing more than just that week?

Wendy had the grace to blush. "I've let my stupid mouth overrun my brain again. I knew I shouldn't have said anything." She rose to leave.

I reached out and grabbed her wrist. "Wendy, I really need to know what Cousin Will Ann was saying. It might have something to do with her murder. We need to know all the facts, the nice and the nasty."

As if there could be any nice. Ouch, that was ugly. But what had Cousin Will Ann said about me this time?

Wendy pursed her lips. "I really couldn't say."

It was fairly obvious that she could say with a bit of coaxing, or maybe some genteel blackmail.

"Tell me," I insisted. "Or I'll write your name in indelible ink on the sign-up sheet to teach the toddlers for the next three quarters. Just as soon as I'm able to get to the church building."

She caved. "Will Ann didn't come right out with it, but she none-too-subtly suggested you were having an affair."

I felt my jaw bounce off the bed. "Me? With who? Whom?"

"She didn't say, but she said she was going to the elders with some interesting information and would insist that they confront you about it."

I swallowed hard. I'd never looked at another man in my entire married life. Jack Bloodworth was my life. Along with my girls. I wouldn't have jeopardized my family for any man, not even one as young and gorgeous as Yanni, much as I loved to listen to his music. And look at his long, black, wavy hair. I jerked myself back to the present.

"I'd like to have seen her try going to the elders. Will Ann certainly didn't have the guts to say it to my face." At least not that I could remember. I thought for a minute. "What, exactly, did she say? What were her very words, if you can remember?"

Wendy frowned in thought. "Something about you being a tramp and a sneak who never believed in the Biblical rule of sex within the bounds of marriage, followed by a snide 'like mother like daughter.' "

"I see," I said, possibly just beginning to see everything. "I don't think she was accusing me of infidelity. She was most likely raking up the old gossip she started umpteen years ago, something about Jack and me eloping because I was pregnant. She called me a tramp and a sneak way back then. Jack and I did elope, but I wasn't pregnant. And she was probably accusing Sunny of sleeping with her precious, innocent, not-to-be-touched-by-my-evil-daughter, baby boy, Craig."

"Oh, dear. How stupid of me. I'd forgotten those old rumors she started about you and Jack back when you two were in high school. Seems like a lifetime ago to me, but probably not to you. Of course that's what she meant. I should've thought of that. I'm sorry if I upset you."

Wendy didn't look all that sorry. "Not at all," I said. "The more we can find out about Cousin Will Ann's last few days, the better chance we have of figuring out who killed her. Lucky for me she's already dead, or I'd strangle her myself."

Wendy grinned at me. "And who would blame you if you did?"

Oh, great. I never should have said that.

"One more thing, Wendy. Exactly when did this confrontation take place?"

"The Wednesday night before she died. I'd gone into the resource room at the church building to get some props for the next Sunday's class. There isn't a whole lot on Ezekiel at the bookstore, you know. But, thankfully, we did have some stuff in a box in the file room."

"And?" At this rate she'd be finishing the story next week.

"Will Ann cornered me in there and demanded to know if I knew who Sunny was sleeping with. I was so horrified, I dropped the Daniel file I'd pulled to check out for the winter quarter, and it scattered stuff all over the floor."

The Daniel file was extremely thick. I had a sudden vision of a paper blizzard. That must have been fun to clean up.

"While I was bending over to gather it all up, she marched out saying that if nobody else had the guts to take care of your family, she would."

"Why didn't you tell me all this before now?"

"I really must go. But, honestly, I couldn't figure out what to do. You know what Will Ann Lloyd was like. She'd charge in for the attack, and before you could return fire she'd be moving on to another target. I thought I should pray about it and talk to you the next time I saw you at church. But by then she was dead, and then you had the accident, and I figured it was best to keep it to myself. I really didn't mean to say anything today but it slipped out. Frankly, it's kept me awake nights."

With that, she grabbed the flowers off my lap and headed toward the door, leaving me staring at her back. "I'll just get the nurse to put these in a vase," she called out from somewhere down the hallway.

So, on Wednesday Cousin Will Ann had accused me of being a tramp and a sneak, and then she'd been murdered just minutes after making the same charges against my Sunny. Okay, how did those accusations tie into her murder? At this point I wasn't sure I really wanted to know.

CHAPTER NINETEEN

I'd been home from the hospital for a couple of days when Cousin Hank stuck his head around the screen door of the sun porch.

Jack and I were enjoying the late afternoon air, snuggling on the futon as I keyed all the important numbers I might need into my new cell phone. Jack had even gone so far as to get each of us a phone, so we could stay in touch whenever we were apart. It wasn't likely that would happen anytime soon since I'd only just recently graduated from wheel chair to crutches, and I still wasn't allowed to drive so he had to take me everywhere.

"Anybody home?" Hank asked.

"Just us chickens," Jack answered, motioning him in.

The rest of Hank's body came onto the back porch, his arm full of flowers. As if I didn't have enough already. Thankfully, Hank's offering appeared to be daisies in a biodegradable pot that would dissolve into the earth after being planted in my kitchen garden just beyond the porch door. Due to the efforts of our caring friends, the container plants on my sun porch had doubled in number since my accident. The porch was beginning to resemble a greenhouse, and I was going to be kept busy watering them all. Not that I minded. One of the reasons I loved the sun porch was because it was like sitting outside, minus the bugs, the hot sun, and the wind.

"Thought these might cheer you up. I know you love daisies," Hank said. He took a seat in my favorite rocking chair and leaned back.

I nodded at him, afraid if I said anything, I'd cry. The support Cousin Will Ann's family had shown me during my recovery had been far greater than I'd ever expected, given that she'd just been murdered and they were still in mourning. Here was Hank, a new widower, and he'd come to the hospital to see me practically every single day. Craig had come to the hospital every day as well, on his way to or from class, and Patricia Ann had usually dropped by in the evening on her way to work. And now Hank had come all the way out to the farm to see us. Must be awfully lonely for him in that big old house in town with Cousin Will Ann gone. I still couldn't seem to wrap my mind around that fact. She'd been so alive, so forceful, I hadn't thought anything could ever stop her. Certainly not a murderer.

I leaned forward, but Jack held me back. "I'll water these for you and I'll bring us all some iced tea."

"That'd be great," Hank said as I nodded.

It was definitely time to think of someone besides myself. "How are you coping, Hank? In the hospital I was too wrapped up in getting well to ask about you. But I'm better now."

"It's hard, not having her there. I can't even sleep in our bedroom. I'm using one of the guest rooms upstairs. Craig is still staying at the house. That's a big help. But tell me more about you."

"I'm on crutches now, to keep most of the weight off my leg, but I am walking. The doctor said I wouldn't."

"He doesn't know you as well as the rest of us, does he?" Hank grinned.

"No, he most surely does not. My ribs are healing, too. Soon I'll be able to use a walker—what fun—with wheels."

Hank winked at me and chuckled. The breeze filtering through the porch screen ruffled his graying hair. Middle-aged or not, Hank Lloyd still had the ability to set female hearts aflutter. My guess was that in another month or so all the single, divorced, or widowed females in and around Massac County would be showing up on his front porch, cakes or casseroles in hand to feed the grieving widower, and with romance on their minds. Nothing wrong with that, as long as a decent mourning period passed before he married again.

I never did hold with the notion that a man who married quickly after his wife died was merely paying tribute to the happy years with her. Hogwash. It made the wife look disposable. I'd always promised Jack Bloodworth I'd haunt him if he so much as looked at another woman in anything under a year after I'd gone. Of course, my real plan was for us to die together, in bed asleep, at a very ripe old age. The accident had very nearly outfoxed me on that one. But I still had hope.

Jack returned with glasses of iced tea, interrupting my thoughts.

"How are things at home, Hank?" Jack asked as he passed out the glasses.

"I've already covered that base," I said. "He's coping. Using the guest bedroom." I turned to Hank. "Have you been able to return to work?"

"Yes, but only part time. Since I own the car lot, 'the boss' is pretty easy on me. But it gets me out of the house. Can't stand to sit around there all day, alone. Craig's at school during the day, and he usually studies with Sunny at night. How are the girls, by the way?"

"Doing fine," Jack said. "Maggie loves the blue van you sold her, and Joe is very grateful for the deal you gave them. They're still bickering with the insurance company because she left the keys in the ignition. But she's happy to have wheels again. I notice she still operates like a NASCAR driver."

And whose fault was that? I let it pass.

"Our grandkids are growing every day," I said. "I swear, while

I was in the hospital, Billy grew a foot."

"You all are lucky to have the little ones around. Helps keep your mind off . . ." Hank's voice trailed off.

I looked at Jack. Yes, we were very lucky. And I wasn't about to forget it.

"I'm so sorry, Hank, that I still don't remember anything about Cousin Will Ann's death or her funeral. It feels disrespectful somehow, but my brain just won't bring it up. It's buried deep in there, somewhere."

"You still can't even remember the accident?" he said. "Seems like something that traumatic wouldn't go away."

I shook my head. "Nope. The very last thing I remember is going to Wal-Mart with Maggie, and Billy throwing up all over the shopping cart. Jack says that happened about a week before Cousin Will Ann died. Everything in-between is either gone, or so hazy I can't call it up."

"Well, I wouldn't worry about it. Like as not, it'll come back when you least expect it." He swallowed a sip of tea.

"I don't know. The doctor thinks it won't. But then, he thought I wouldn't walk again either." I grinned and tipped my glass towards Jack's in a mock toast. We clanged glasses.

"I have more faith in you than the doctor," Jack said as Hank nodded agreement.

"Hank, is there anything we can do to help you through this?" I asked.

"Just give me time and lots of prayers," he replied.

That was a given. The three of us settled back more comfortably to listen to the late afternoon sounds. Living on a sixty acre farm way out in the county had its perks. No city traffic noises, and no other buildings to look at except our own. Plus, the pond full of catfish just off to my left. The clouds were large and purple, maybe a coming storm? I snuggled back under Jack's arm and watched.

This kind of storm I enjoyed. But what kind of storm would we all face when Cousin Will Ann's murderer was caught? And what if he and or she never was caught?

Which would ultimately be worse?

Chapter Twenty

After Hank left, Jack insisted we walk out to the pole barn.

"You can't avoid it forever, Kitty. The Paducah Police Department released Sadie back to me while you were still in the hospital. Joe drove her home for me."

I reached for my crutches, still not as steady on them as I'd like. "Okay. Let's go."

Jack stopped at the edge of the pole barn, and we stood there watching the sun as it dropped behind the trees surrounding our pond. A goose, obviously lost, honked as he zoomed overhead, then settled into a soft landing on the calm water. He continued to honk as if to encourage his friends—wherever they were—to join him. I took a deep breath of fresh air.

Jack turned to me. "I know I said I was going to sell Sadie, but I've changed my mind."

Sell our beautiful Chevy? When had he said that? And why would he? He loved that car. It allowed him to go back to a place in time when the world around us seemed so much simpler.

"I want us to get our lives back to where they were before Will Ann's murder and your accident. Wonderfully normal and boring," Jack continued. "I very nearly lost you, and I still don't see how you found the courage to survive for a whole night and day inside that wreck."

"Easy," I responded. "I knew if I'd died in there, Maggie would insist on putting up one of those dreadful plastic funeral arrangements along the roadside, probably right where I went off, in honor of my memory. And I wouldn't put it past her to have my name painted on the wooden easel, for all the world to read. And to wonder why I'd been so stupid as to run off the road where no one could find me. I didn't figure you or Sunny would have the courage to stop her."

Jack laughed, a mighty welcome sound after the long days of my recovery. "Truth is, she hinted at it that first night at the hospital, but she backed down when I threatened to take my belt off to her."

"Like you ever whipped her with a belt in her entire life! Not that she didn't need it. But the girls had you wrapped around their little fingers from day one."

"I know, just like you have me wrapped." He gave me a gentle hug. "Come on, you have to face this sooner or later."

Jack unlocked and slid the huge double doors open, and we stepped into the cavernous wood and metal barn. He flipped a switch and the barn lit up like a high school gymnasium. Thirty feet wide by forty feet long, the metal sides were supported by treated poles that met twenty feet in the air to support the metal roof. Not one to skimp on the essentials, Jack had run water pipes as well as electricity service to his beloved barn. Of course it was heated and air conditioned. Nothing but the best for our Sadie. The concrete floor radiated cool air around us. Jack's many trophies and antique car collectibles gleamed from the shelves he'd built to house them. At least he'd soon be finished with the shelves in the garage.

I glanced at Sadie and a shiver ran up my legs and did an electrified dance across my shoulder blades. I was thankful I still couldn't remember seeing Cousin Will Ann's face frozen in death. I sincerely hoped that part of my memory never returned.

Jack opened Sadie's trunk and guided me over to it.

"Maybe seeing this will help stop your nightmares."

"Seeing what?" The trunk of the old Chevy was cleaner than my guest bedroom carpet, not a speck of dust or a stray hair. The Paducah Police Department hadn't left anything behind to show that a body had ever been hidden in our trunk. I reached out and ran my hand over the carpet. The smell of air freshener floated up to my nostrils.

"Do you suppose Will Ann suffered?" I asked.

Jack looked me in the eye, fully prepared to lie, but apparently saw that I wouldn't accept anything but the plain, unvarnished truth and gave it to me. "Yes, she would have suffered terribly for a few minutes. But the killer grabbed her from behind, so it's unlikely she saw who it was."

At least she'd been spared that, particularly if it was someone she knew and trusted.

There was really nothing to see in the trunk, and thankfully, no ghosts, although I wouldn't have put it past Will Ann Lloyd to haunt our car, out of spite.

When Jack first bought the car, it had been in pretty bad shape. Which was exactly what he'd wanted. But Cousin Will Ann's tongue was as sharp as my best paring knife, full of jabs about "old boys and their toys," not to mention my stupidity for letting him "play." And defending myself against her jabs always produced defensive wounds. Wounds that were just as painful as a real-life knife attack would've been. When Jack finally finished the restoration and started winning trophies with the car, you'd have thought she'd let up on him.

That certainly didn't happen.

So, why did we tolerate her? Because she was family and we didn't just dump family no matter how tacky they sometimes acted. Not without extenuating reasons. And we didn't have so much family that we could afford to toss out a whole bushel basket because of one bad apple.

I crutched my way around Sadie, looking for dings and

bumps, and was very thankful not to find any. The interior of the car was still as pristine as the outside. Obviously, the crime scene techs knew a piece of art when they saw one. I said a quick prayer of thanks for the CSI techs.

Jack raised the hood to show me that the engine was as clean and shiny as a baby's bottom after bath time. He reached around inside the driver's window, turned the key, and the glass packs gave their usual satisfying pop as the engine roared to life. I leaned over the fender and watched him tinker here and there, tightening this, checking that, and was happy to see him back to normal. Just like when we were dating and I helped him work on his car.

He turned off the engine, came to my side of the car, and put his arms around me.

"What say we get in the back seat and make this baby really rock and roll?" He wiggled his eyebrows in that cute, suggestive way. "I promise, I'll be gentle with your broken parts."

I glanced at the back seat. Following his suggestion certainly would chase away any lingering bad vibes from the murder. And I'd always wondered if it really was that much fun to make out in the back seat of a car.

"Might as well be hung for a goat as a sheep," Jack said.

"Does that still bother you?" I asked,

"Of course it still bothers me. Your cousin Will Ann was making out with half the guys on the football team. The locker room pun, or play on her name, was 'Who Will Ann sleep with next?' But she always managed to keep the spotlight on someone else and away from herself."

Straight-laced, sophisticated Will Ann Halliburton had made out with half the football team? Who knew?

"And there you and I were," Jack said, interrupting my thoughts, "just scrounging for some change under the back seat of my car to get a little Coke money and Will Ann sees us and runs to your mother. And we wind up having to sneak off to another state to get married."

Actually, she'd run with her story about us to her mother, who'd run to my mother, who'd forbidden me, with my father's blessings, to ever see or speak to Jack Bloodworth again.

Jack scratched the bridge of his nose. "I know how much you wanted a proper wedding, with all your friends as bridesmaids, and your father giving you away. I've never forgiven Will Ann for that. Or myself," Jack added.

And all because Cousin Will Ann said she'd caught us in a compromising position at a drive-in movie, lo those many moons ago. I was underage and seeing no other viable options, Jack and I had sneaked off and gotten married in a state with a lower age requirement so my parents couldn't have it annulled. The dehumidifier kicked on, regulating the moisture in the large barn and keeping Jack's collection safe from rust, at least for now.

"I'm glad we went ahead and got married even though I was still in high school," I said. "Of course, I wouldn't have wanted that for our girls, or for Tori. I'm glad Maggie had the good sense to finish college before she got married and had Tori and Billy. And Sunny is still waiting for the right man to come along. But times are different now. Our generation matured much quicker than theirs. We had to."

Jack nodded. "But you missed out on the celebration for the most important day of your life. We didn't even have a reception."

"No, I didn't miss out. It was more important for me to be with you. Getting married gave me that. It wasn't important what I wore, or who was there. Besides, it was romantic, slipping off like that."

Jack didn't look convinced. "But it changed your relationship with your folks forever. They never forgave either one of us. And

I've never stopped feeling guilty for that."

I touched his arm. "Jack Bloodworth, marrying you is the smartest thing I ever did. Yes, we were stupid to get pregnant on our wedding night. It convinced my parents that Cousin Will Ann was telling the truth about us. But my mother should have believed me when I told her we'd waited to get married before having sex and that Will Ann was just trying to break us up."

The large old barn creaked and groaned, settling down for the night. I pinched my nose, not wanting him to see that I was about to cry. "Truth to tell, Mother cared more about what Will Ann's mother, Aunt Ann thought, and keeping up appearances with her, than she ever cared about me. That still hurts, and I made sure that kind of disloyalty never happened between me and my daughters. But it was Mother's choice to keep her distance from us, not ours. It was her loss. We've made it just fine."

"Yeah, but if we'd waited, we could've gone straight to college after graduation, instead of me going to night school and you having to wait until we could afford it. And we could've moved into a place of our own instead of living with my parents until I got a decent job."

We'd had this discussion before. About a trillion times.

"And if we'd waited, you probably wouldn't have lost the baby," Jack said. "The doctor insisted that you were way too young to give birth. He blamed me for that."

Jack gently kicked Sadie's back tire. This part of the discussion we'd never had. Far too painful.

"Dr. Baker couldn't possibly have known that for certain, and neither could we. Maybe I didn't take proper care of myself during the pregnancy," I said, wondering if I had. "Or maybe it was because my body hadn't developed enough to carry our son. Who knows? It could be that Dr. Baker said it because he'd been friends with my parents for years and knew how angry they were with me for running off with you. As a way to punish us. Whatever the reason, it's no use blaming ourselves now." I leaned down and kissed his cheek.

"Besides," I said, "I never minded living with your mom and dad. They treated me like a daughter. I had to make a choice between you and my parents, Jack, and I've never once regretted the results. Now, let's see if there is any change behind that back seat."

I crawled slowly through Sadie's passenger door, with a bit of a push from Jack, and quickly discovered heaven in the back seat of a '57 Chevy.

It was something I'd always suspected Cousin Will Ann had discovered for herself way back in high school. But she'd somehow managed to keep that fact hidden from her mother, not to mention mine.

I also discovered that Jack Bloodworth probably had cancer.

Chapter Twenty-One

"Why didn't you tell me you had a knot the size of Mount McKinley on your groin?" I demanded.

He ducked his head, a sure sign a lie was on it's way out of his mouth. Jack Bloodworth was the world's worst liar. Next to me, that is.

"Didn't want to scare you."

Right.

"I'm not scared," I fudged back, "But I'm haulin' your hinny to the doctor first thing tomorrow morning."

He patted his pocket for a cigarette, remembered he'd stopped smoking right after Sunny was born, and reached over to ruffle my hair instead. "No need to haul me anywhere. I made an appointment with Dr. Morrison over in Paducah some time ago. Had to cancel while you were laid up in the hospital, but they rescheduled me for a week from yesterday."

I swallowed hard. He'd made his own appointment? This must be really serious.

"Why didn't you tell me this before?"

"Didn't want you to worry."

Uh huh.

Jack looked into my eyes and apparently decided to level with me. "The truth is, I figured I'd had it. I wasn't planning on seeing the doctor at all. I was just going to let nature take its course. No chemo, no radiation. I avoided touching you, so you wouldn't see the knot, but I could see that by hiding it I was hurting you, so I thought maybe I'd best do something about it after all."

I leaned against the back passenger window. He'd been avoiding me? In the bedroom? I'd been so wrapped up in the pain of the accident and the recovery process, I'd put that problem completely out of my mind. Had I done anything about it before the accident? This short term memory loss thing was really causing problems with my daily life. Better to remember the bad times so I could deal with them, and I certainly never wanted to lose any of my good memories.

Jack helped me out of the back seat, something I was none too graceful at even in the best of times, and we went inside to bed. He held me tight all night long. The thought of life without him was not to be borne. We cried, and we prayed, and finally we fell asleep.

Thursday morning I dressed, slowly and carefully, as always. I'd graduated to the walker, just like some ninety-nine-year-old blue hair, but once therapy ended I could try a cane until my leg fully healed. Not one of those cold-looking, hospital issued, metal thingies, but a nicely carved number with a rubber tip for safety. I'd go antiquing with Debby as soon as I could and find a beautiful old cane that was much loved and well broken in by someone before me. So much for the squeamishness Debby said I'd been exhibiting recently about using the belongings of the dearly departed.

I'd been reminded of one or two important life lessons by Cousin Will Ann's murder and my accident. Possessions did indeed outlive people, and it didn't matter what happened to those possessions or which people possessed them after the owners were gone. What mattered was whether or not the owner was missed because she'd been valuable, not her possessions.

We arrived at the doctor's office way too early, and I thought

I might have to tie Jack into a chair in the waiting room. I let him pace while I thumbed an old magazine and kept an eye on the door in case he bolted for it. At long last the nurse leaned back on the door of the inner sanctum and called Jack's name in a voice that would have made our pigs jump for the slop trough if we'd still had any. I scooted my walker into the hallway close behind him, fearing she'd try to keep me out. She gave me a look but let me pass.

The doctor examined Jack and asked several questions, getting grunts for responses much of the time.

"Mr. Bloodworth, you can get dressed, and my nurse will show you to my office." He turned and looked me up and down as if to determine whether or not Jack might be responsible for my physical condition. I gave him my best smile to reassure him I was fine and dandy, despite the knot in my stomach.

Seated in front of the doctor's huge desk, I glanced around at his diplomas, needing reassurance that he had the brains and the training to heal my husband. The schools he'd gone to seemed to think so. Well, we'd see.

Dr. Morrison entered the room, Jack's file in hand, and swept into the large chair behind his desk. I bit my tongue to keep from firing off questions before he'd settled into place, and wondered who watered the ivy trailing down the bookcase behind his head. A rather large bowling ball rolled around inside my stomach, searching for pins to knock over.

"Mr. Bloodworth," the good doctor began. I waited, feeling like the bank president was about to say he was foreclosing on our farm. "The knot in your groin could be cancer, but it may well not be. We won't know until we go in. But with it being situated in such close proximity to several lymph glands, I suggest we remove it as soon as possible. I'll send it off for biopsy and then we'll know what we're dealing with."

Jack and I looked at each other and nodded at the doctor,

too afraid to speak. I'd thought he'd be able to tell if it was cancerous or not just by examining Jack. I hadn't expected to have to wait several more days for answers. I hadn't minded being patient throughout my own recovery and physical therapy, or waiting to find out if I'd ever walk again. Waiting to see whether or not Jack was going to live or die would be about as much fun as defusing an atom bomb. And just about as easy.

"I'll have my nurse call the hospital and schedule the surgery for the earliest possible moment. I don't want us to wait on this." The doctor looked over his glasses at Jack. "You know, you really should have come to see me as soon as you found the knot, Mr. Bloodworth. It's never safe to put these things off."

Jack had the grace to duck his head. "Is this surgery going to affect our, ummm . . ." He waved his hands around, trying to come up with the proper words.

People of our generation didn't usually say the word "sex" out loud in mixed company. Certainly not in the company of strangers, despite the ease with which it was bandied about in movies and on television these days. I decided to bail him out. "What he means is, can we still have sex?"

Dr. Morrison blinked at me and looked pointedly at my walker again. Bet he thought the older generation was a bunch of sissies who gave up sex at the first hint of a handicap.

Our parents hadn't survived two World Wars and the Depression for nothing. And the lesson they'd handed down to us, the generation now known as baby boomers, was: You're as young as you feel. I still felt like I was in my thirties, even if my body occasionally refused to cooperate. And these new young professional guys probably hadn't paid enough attention in history class to learn the same lesson. As a surgeon, often dealing with older patients, he should know better.

"No, this shouldn't affect your personal relationship in that area at all, although you will be sore for quite some time after the surgery and may have to wait until you heal, Mr. Blood-worth."

He smiled at me. Okay, so he had paid attention in high school. Score one for the doc.

Jack thanked him and headed for the door with me slowly bringing up the rear. I was exhausted from worry and lack of sleep and still none too steady on my new wheels.

The girl at the desk gave Jack a print-out telling him where to be in one week, what to do when he got there, and what not to eat before he came. We went home to wait. And pray.

CHAPTER TWENTY-TWO

"There's really nothing else we haven't told you about Cousin Will Ann's murder. Honest, Mom," Maggie assured me.

We were drinking tea and enjoying the view of the pond from my sun porch. I'd finished putting photos in the family album that morning—a job I'd been putting off for over a year and now had no clue as to the time line of the more recent pictures. Over the last few days I'd cleaned out my desk several times. I tried to read a new mystery novel and wasn't able to make sense of it at all. I worried about Jack and wondered who had killed Cousin Will Ann. And why.

While I'd been recovering in the hospital, Dr. Twerp urged my family not to discuss with me any details about Cousin Will Ann's murder, fearing that in my delicate state I couldn't handle it. Delicate, schmelicate, that boy needed nothing so much as a smack upside the head. At my insistence they'd told me what they knew anyway, and we'd gone over it several times. Nothing my family said thus far had jogged my memory.

"Except I forgot to mention that you were pretty skeptical of Sunny and Craig's story—that they were studying together—because apparently she first told you she'd spent the evening alone," Maggie said. "They've always been very close, despite the fact that Cousin Will Ann didn't encourage her kids to play with us. It wouldn't surprise me at all if they lied for each other."

"Wouldn't surprise me either," I said, and took another bite of a delicious peanut butter cookie. Maggie knew I liked anything with peanut butter in it or on it. Her peanut butter cookies were equaled by none.

My granddaughter Tori played quietly in the corner with her mother's old doll house, and Billy was out in the garage with Grandpa. Jack had finished the new shelves in the garage and was now carefully storing all of my decorations where I could reach them, once I was well enough. I'm also big on Halloween, Easter and the Fourth of July.

The lack of outraged screams from either party reassured me that those two were probably enjoying each other's company, at least for the moment. Before long they'd be out at the pond, skipping rocks. Typical guy thing. Except Tori was a pretty decent rock-skipper, as well, thanks to her grandpa. No telling what else he taught the kids when their mother wasn't looking. Or me.

"Detective Parker came to see me a couple of times in the hospital," I said, between bites. "Until Dr. Twining finally convinced him that I really did not remember a thing about Cousin Will Ann's death or my accident. Dr. Twining was extremely gleeful to be of help to the detective. Perhaps a bit too much so, if you ask me." I took another sip of tea.

"At least he kept the good detective from bothering you. Parker's called me nearly every single day since your accident, as if he's trying to catch me in a lie or something."

"I hope he doesn't break Sunny down, assuming she isn't telling the truth about being with Craig that night. I need a chance to talk with her first. Not that she'll open up to me any better than she has to Detective Parker."

I thought about that for a minute. "She's been avoiding me since I came home. I've invited her to dinner tonight. I still have a casserole and a pie in the fridge, left over from when the girls at church activated the meal list to help your dad out while I was in the hospital. I bet old Pharaoh himself didn't have a storehouse as full as my pantry when the drought hit Egypt."

Maggie smiled. "What would we do without our friends to help us?"

What, indeed? Debby had driven to the farm nearly every day since I'd come home, helping me bathe and take care of a few other intimate female chores. Sunny offered, but I didn't want her to miss any more classes, and help from Maggie would've involved having my grandchildren's assistance too. I hadn't recovered nearly enough for that. I wondered how we'd manage with Jack's surgery.

"There's something else I need to talk to both you and Sunny about." I lowered my voice and looked over my shoulder to make sure Tori was still engrossed in Barbie and Ken and not sneaking up on Scheherazade. Schadzie wisely watched Tori from a safe distance on a window sill.

"Your father has a tumor in his groin area. He's scheduled for surgery on Tuesday. That's the soonest they could get him in at the hospital. I think—"

Whatever I thought was forever lost in Maggie's enveloping hug and my tears. She held me while I sobbed like a baby, swallowing the sounds so Tori wouldn't hear.

"I'll call Etta Strong and tell her to put Dad on the prayer list. You guys should've told us about this sooner."

"I only found out a couple of days ago," I stuttered. "He made an appointment without telling me, then cancelled it after the accident. If it's cancer, there's no telling how far it's spread while he sat day after day with me at the hospital. If I hadn't been playing cop, chasing your van—"

"Nobody knows if you were truly chasing my van, and if that's the case, then I'm to blame too, for leaving my keys in the van. Remember, you forbade me to feel guilty about your accident, so you can't blame yourself for Dad putting off his appointment. Not without blaming me. You can't have it both ways."

Tori propped a doll in a miniature wicker chair and headed for the cookie plate on the table in front of us. Must be tea party time. I quickly dried my eyes.

"You're right. Things happen. We just have to learn to live with them. I'll let you know what I find out from Sunny tonight. In fact, why don't you all come to dinner too? We can talk in the kitchen, over the dirty dishes."

"Tori, you're going to gag yourself. Don't put more than one cookie in your mouth at a time. And save some for your brother and Gramps." Maggie turned her attention back to me. "Good idea, Mom. Joe has to work overtime, so I wasn't planning on cooking a big meal. What time do you want us, and what can I bring?"

"Six. Salad and rolls."

She gathered up her brood to head home. A nap for the children and possibly a nap for herself would go a long way toward a peaceful dinner this evening. And it wouldn't be amiss for me to have a nap, either, assuming I could relax and turn off the questions in my head about Jack's future.

And about who was lying to protect whom. Craig or Sunny?

CHAPTER TWENTY-THREE

Dinner was a success, quizzing Sunny was not. Where was Parker's rubber hose when you really needed it?

Sunny stuck to her story about being with Craig the night his mother was killed like chewing gum to the underside of an elementary school desk. Where had she learned such stubbornness?

Rhetorical question.

"I'll have to get Betty's recipe for that casserole," Sunny said, as she dried the last glass and put it in the cabinet.

Maggie was wiping off the counters while I supervised from a nearby chair. Judging by the noises coming from the living room, there was a bull-riding contest going on, with grandpa as the bull.

"I'll get it for you," I said. "Stop evading me, young lady. I need the truth."

"Mom, I told you the truth, Craig and I were together."

"Say 'beans' without smiling and I'll know you're telling me the truth."

Both girls burst into giggles, just like they always had when they were little and trying to wiggle out of something.

"Mom, Craig did not kill his mother. Neither did I. Let's leave it at that. Besides, I don't care what Detective Parker says, I'll never believe anyone in this family killed Cousin Will Ann. It had to be some maniac."

"Honey, your dad and I are convinced it had to be someone

who knows our family. Why else would they put her in our car? Which, incidentally, was locked up tight in our pole barn."

Sunny shook her head.

"I'd like to believe it was some passing stranger as well," I said, "but we can't shut our eyes to this. We have to know who killed her. And I don't think Detective Parker is going to solve it."

"Why not?" Maggie asked. "He seems pretty sharp to me."

"I'm sure he is, but don't you ever watch 'The First 48' on the A & E channel? According to that show, if the police don't have a solid suspect within the first forty-eight hours, the case usually goes cold. We're way past that deadline," I said.

"You watch too much television, Mother," Sunny said. "Speaking of passing strangers, particularly of the handsome variety, have you looked at Scheherazade lately? My guess is she's had another romantic encounter."

I looked down at Schadzie, eating daintily out of her bowl, and had to admit her belly was dragging the ground even more than usual. I really needed to have her spayed. We'd pretty much run out of friends to palm her kittens off on.

"Nice try, Sunshine," I said, "but you aren't getting out of this discussion."

"Mom, I've said all I'm going to say. Either you believe me or you don't. I thought you said you weren't going to be like your mother?"

Perish the thought. Best to let it drop. For now. I'd have to try something else. Like maybe tackling Craig.

But I'd have to make sure Sunny didn't find out. Or I really would be dead.

Tackling Craig proved to be a bit tougher than I'd thought. After Sunny and Maggie each left for home, one to study, the other to bathe children and warm a plate for a late-working hubby, I called and invited Craig over for pie and coffee. It was handy having him back in Metropolis rather than over an hour away in Carbondale. Somehow, I'd have to figure out how to keep him from telling Sunny about this little impromptu visit.

"Craig, are you telling me the truth about you and Sunny spending the evening together the night your mother was killed?" We were sitting out on the sun porch, which had barely begun to cool from the day's warm sun pouring in.

"Yes, Cousin Kitty. I'm telling you the truth. We were together that whole evening."

So why wasn't he making eye contact when he said that? I didn't want to push too hard, but I'd known this kid a very long time. He was hiding something. But what?

"Craig, if there's anything you want to tell me, now is the time. I'm not going to share it with Detective Parker, particularly if it's something that will hurt Sunny. Or you."

He shook his head. "Honest, there's nothing to tell. Sunny couldn't have hurt my mother."

He still wasn't looking straight at me, but seemed to be fascinated with something just over my left shoulder. I didn't bother to turn around.

"Would you have any idea who did kill your mother?" Might as well see if I could shake anything else loose.

He gave the question serious consideration then said, "My first thought was of Hank. I know he was crazy about Mother, but he had to be at the top of the list. I was actually relieved when I found out he'd been at the chamber meeting."

Craig studied his shoes for a minute or two. "I know Mother was hard to deal with, but I just can't figure out who killed her. And I can't imagine why you keep questioning me or Sunny. We told you where we were."

"I assume Sunny told you what your mother said to us when she blew into Farley's the night she died?"

"Just that Mother was looking for her and was upset about

something. I figured it was the same old thing, her wanting to see if we were dating. We weren't."

I had a sudden light-bulb-over-the-head moment. "But you'd like to be dating Sunny, wouldn't you?"

He kept studying his shoes.

"Craig?"

"Actually, I'd like to spend the rest of my life with her. I've been in love with Sunny since middle school. She doesn't suspect. But these last few months, studying together so much, has been a lovely kind of torture for me. She says there isn't anyone else, but she keeps me at friend's length."

"Friend's length?"

"Yeah, just slightly farther than arm's length."

"And she told you there's no one else?"

He nodded. "You think I'd ever have a chance with her, Cousin Kitty?"

"Maybe," I said. "She followed you like a lost puppy when you were both in first grade."

"Yeah, I remember. Just wish I'd had more sense back then. We might be married by now, if I hadn't told her over and over how yucky I thought girls were. I didn't wake up until eighth grade, and by then she'd fallen for somebody else."

I laughed.

"It was hard, losing my mother that way, but I swear, neither Sunny nor I were involved."

Maybe I should share everything with Craig since Sunny obviously hadn't. "The reason I keep pushing this is because when your mother showed up at Farley's that night, she accused Sunny of being a tramp and a sneak. Your mother was a harsh woman, but she'd never said anything like that about Sunny before. What could she have meant?"

Craig stood and clenched his fists. "I don't know, but if she were still alive I'd find out. It certainly isn't true. Sunny's an angel. My mother had no business saying that."

" 'No business' never stopped her from speaking her mind."

"I know. Mom could cut people off at the knees sometimes. I'm just surprised she attacked Sunny. Mom didn't have a problem with Sunny until recently."

Jack stepped onto the sun porch and wiped his hands on an old rag. He'd decided to give the Chevy a final rub-down before locking up the pole barn for the night. After the surgery the doctor wasn't going to allow him out there for several days.

"Is my backside clean? Can I sit down?" he asked.

I dusted him off, leaving out the usual flirtatious pinch so as not to shock Craig's youthful sensibilities. Whoever said youth was wasted on the young had most likely raised teenagers and dealt with them as young adults at some point.

"How are you, Craig?" Jack asked, plopping onto the futon beside me. Craig sat down again.

"I'm doing okay, Cousin Jack. I guess it will take me a while to get used to the fact that my mother was murdered. And deal with the anger." He punched a fist into his open palm. "Man, I wish Detective Parker would solve the case. I really can't get on with my life until he does."

"Neither can we," Jack and I said in unison. Jack grinned at me.

Craig stood to leave, reached for Jack's hand, and gave it a firm shake. "I appreciate everything you folks have done for us since . . . well, since, you-know. If there's ever anything I can do for you two, just ask."

Jack stood up and said, "Thanks." Then he paused for several seconds and jingled the change in his pocket. Finally, he looked at Craig. "I know this is a bad time for you, but I'd like you to help Joe keep an eye on Kitty and my girls, in case they need you. I'll be having surgery soon." Jack glanced at me. "Might turn out to be cancer, might not."

I felt a chill on the warm porch and folded my arms across my shoulders.

"I'm sorry to hear that, Cousin Jack," Craig said, startled. Then, emphatically, "You bet I'll keep an eye on them."

Craig waved as he pushed through the porch door. I called after him, "Craig, can we keep this visit between us? Sunny is already mad at me."

"Sure thing, Cousin Kitty. She won't hear anything from me. And thanks for the pie. It was delicious, as always." He disappeared around the corner of the house.

I put my tea glass down, picked up Shahdzie, and handed her to Jack to put outside for her evening stroll. When he came back, I patted the futon seat.

"Sit with me for a bit. I'm not real sleepy right now," I said.

"Happy to, if you give me some of that tea. Wiping down a car is thirsty work."

I reached for another glass on the tray and poured for him. We sat in silence and listened to the insects gearing up for their nightly chorus with the frogs at the pond. One particularly vigorous frog always sounded as though he was daring the others to match his volume and enthusiasm. So far none had.

"You nervous about the surgery?" I asked.

Jack swallowed a sip and looked out at the pond. I knew he was thinking of the other evening when we'd "christened" the back seat of the Chevy in the pole barn.

"No need to be nervous," he finally said. "Either it's cancer, or it isn't. No use borrowing trouble. Trouble comes in its own time."

I hated it when he philosophized about things that scared me silly.

"Then why did you ask Craig to keep an eye on me and the kids? You know Joe would step in and take care of the girls, and me, if that was ever necessary."

"Wanted Craig to know he's still part of the family in spite of the fact that you think he and Sunny are lying."

I thought that over. "Good idea. Incidentally, I got our cancer policy out today, just in case. Whatever happens," I promised, "you are going to get the best possible care."

He did the eyebrow lift. "Does that include my physical needs?"

I slapped his arm with the magazine I'd been reading earlier. "Not until we've had another piece of pie. No use letting it go to waste."

I wasn't hungry in the least, but I couldn't sit still any longer. Soon my whole life might be upside down. It was already tilting seriously, like a rogue planet blown off it's axis, by Cousin Will Ann's murder. And my accident. And Jack's upcoming surgery. I wondered if the bowling ball in my stomach would ever dissolve.

CHAPTER TWENTY-FOUR

"Grandma, my tooth accidentally fell into my ear," Tori announced.

I opened my eyes and sighed. I'd finish my prayer for Jack's safe recovery just as soon as I'd dealt with my granddaughter. Tori stood in front of me, elbows on my knees, staring straight up into my eyes.

"Grandma, did you hear me?"

I was pretty sure most of the third floor of the hospital had heard her, if not the second as well. Other occupants of the chairs and couches had turned to stare. Before I could answer Tori, Maggie strode into the surgical waiting area, blowing stray bangs out of her eyes, with Billy riding just above the bulky wad of T-shirt on her hip.

"I'm so sorry, Mom. I would've been here on time, but for a slight detour to the ER with Tori. Joe will be here later, if he can. They needed him to work for a couple of hours. Some problem only the foreman could handle." She passed Billy, complete with sippy cup, to Sunny, who was seated to my left, watching the morning news on the television mounted in the corner. Maggie squished down beside me on the vinyl couch, and doubled over. For a minute, I thought she was crying. A closer look told me she was shaking with laughter.

"What were you doing in the ER, Maggie? Was one of the kids hurt, or sick?" I assumed they must be at least marginally okay or she wouldn't be here in the first place, but I was still bumfuzzled as to what was going on.

With her hand covering her mouth, the way mothers do when they don't want their children to know they're laughing at them, Maggie said, "Tori, tell Grammy about your tooth. I don't think she heard you the first time."

I looked across to Sunny, but she appeared to be as puzzled as I was. Tori tugged on my blouse.

"Grandma, my tooth accidentally fell into my ear."

I swallowed hard on a giggle. "Okay, how, exactly, did your tooth fall into your ear?"

"Well, I lost my front tooth this morning. See?" She opened her mouth and pointed to the now-empty space.

"In case you're interested, it was her lateral incisor, according to the emergency room nurse," Maggie put in.

Tori turned and pointed to her baby brother. "Billy knocked it out. He didn't mean to. He was climbing down off the bathroom sink and I was helping him. His foot hit my mouth, and my tooth fell out. It's been loose for a long time, so it wasn't really his fault."

Sibling loyalty. How long would that last?

"Is that how it got into your ear?" I asked, doubtfully.

Tori turned her attention back to me. "Of course not, Grandma. Don't be silly. Mommy wiped the blood off of it. Then she picked up Billy, to change his diaper. It was awful." She waved her hand in front of her nose to demonstrate just how serious the diaper situation had been.

I nodded, having been on the front line at the changing table many times when the odor from Billy's diaper rivaled the county dump on a hot July day.

"And," I prompted, fascinated and wanting to hear the rest of this story.

"Well, Mommy was busy with Billy, and my ear itched, so I tried to scratch it with my tooth. But it fell inside, and when I tried to get it out, it went in more. Mommy said I had to go to the hospital. But I was very brave. I didn't even cry," she assured me.

Sunny snickered and Tori gave her aunt a suspicious look. Sunny immediately straightened her face and Tori continued her tale of woe.

"The doctor got it out, with a little plastic thing that they keep here for kids like me. He said they see this all the time."

Teeth in the ear? All the time?

"She means kids poking things smaller than their elbows into their ears, Mom," Maggie said, reading my mind. "From the look on the emergency room doctor's face, I suspect this was the first tooth he'd retrieved out of an ear."

"But Mommy," Tori said, "elbows don't fit inside your ear. That's a silly saying."

"It isn't a silly saying at all," I argued. "Particularly since you stuck your tooth into your ear. I always taught the 'nothing smaller than your elbow' rule to my kindergarteners, and none of them ever went to the hospital with a tooth in their ears. Maybe you need to remember it."

Tori ducked her head. "Yes, Grandma."

"I tried to call you, Mom, to let you know I'd be late, but Billy was yelling for his breakfast and Tori was sobbing even louder because she was afraid it would hurt when they removed the tooth from inside her ear, and she was convinced that the Tooth Fairy wouldn't come if she didn't have the tooth to put under her pillow, and she thought you would spank her. Besides that, your cell phone isn't on."

The sound of my cell phone ringing was always so unexpected it made my knickers wad. I only turned it on when I absolutely had to make a call. Which wasn't often. So I ignored the last part of Maggie's explanation and turned to Tori.

"Young lady, when was the last time Grammy even threatened

to spank you, much less actually did it?"

She thought that over. "When I pulled Schadzie's tail."

"Yes, that's true, but I didn't actually spank you, did I? Because you promised never to pull her tail again."

"And when I accidentally steered Grandpa's truck into the garage door while he was teaching me to drive. You threatened to spank both of us that time. Grandpa didn't seem very scared, but I sure was."

She had me there. I noticed Maggie's eyes narrow. We generally dealt with Maggie on a "need to know" basis. If she didn't need to know all the details of her children's visits to our home, we certainly didn't share them. Saved us a lot of lectures on child rearing. Jack always swore she'd forgotten who'd raised her.

I carefully lifted Tori up into my lap, partly to reassure her, and partly to keep her from relating more incidents before my daughter assumed I was either abusing or leading astray her innocent young children. Actually, all abuse and leading astray generally went in the other direction. Jack and I were left totally exhausted after a day with our grandchildren. I generally felt far younger than my birth certificate indicated, until we spent time entertaining Tori and Billy.

"I wouldn't have spanked you for something like this." I stopped just short of adding or anything else. No use blowing my cover as a hard-nosed grandma before I had to.

"You've already figured out that it didn't hurt to have the tooth taken out of your ear, and even if it had been lost, the Tooth Fairy would still come. So you worried about nothing, didn't you?" This from the greatest worrier of all. I was afraid to look at my daughters.

Tori nodded, and Billy's small voice, from the seat to my left, chimed in. "Grammy, how would the Tooth Fairy know to come to our house if Tori didn't have the tooth under her pillow?

Everyone knows you have to have a tooth under your pillow for her to come."

Trust a two year old to go to the heart of the matter. I took a deep breath. Telling tall tales was never easy for me. "The Tooth Fairy not only looks for teeth under pillows, she looks for empty spaces in your mouth as well."

"But how does she know there is a empty space in your mouth? How about Grandpa? He has lots of empty spaces in his mouth. I saw 'em when he took his teeth out to brush 'em. How come Grandpa can take his teeth out and I can't?"

Fortunately, I was saved from answering when Hank stepped into the waiting room. He carried a cardboard tray loaded with Starbucks coffee and a box of donuts. Craig was close behind. I put Tori down and stood to hug Hank and Craig. I couldn't eat or even have a cup of coffee in front of Jack earlier this morning, not when he wasn't allowed to have anything. And now I was starving.

"How's Jack?" Hank asked, as he eased himself into a chair beside me and placed the goodies on a small table.

"No word, yet," I answered as he passed me a steaming cup.

"It's decaf," Hank said. "I know how wired you get from caffeine."

"Thanks." The warm cup felt good in my stiff hands.

He passed Craig and Maggie a cup, but Sunny declined. She scooped Billy back up into her arms and said, "Let's go for a walk, fella." He squirmed down and headed for Hank.

"No, I wanna donut. I bet Cousin Hank brought chocolate filled." He gave Hank his most charming grin, the one he generally used to get grandpa to take him for a ride on our big green tractor.

"Chocolate crème filled," Hank corrected, and he reached into the box and came out with the prize.

"Me, too," Tori insisted, joining her brother at the table.

Hank produced yet another of the coveted donuts. I was afraid Maggie was going to yank the box out of Hank's hand, but she merely leaned over, staring at him until he passed her the box. She politely passed me a glazed and pounced on the last crème filled. I'm nobody's fool. My eldest daughter wasn't being polite so much as she was getting the dross out of the way so she could get down to her favorite.

Sunny waved the box away. What was wrong with that girl? She adored donuts. Not to mention Starbucks coffee.

"I've put on five pounds this month, just by studying so much with Craig." Sunny winked at the poor, lovesick boy, and he blushed. "He always wants to order a pizza. I've simply got to cut back."

With the donut half-way to my mouth, I noticed she'd made the rest of her statement directly to Hank, with a slight tilt to her chin, as if daring him to object to the time she was spending with his stepson. I sighed. Tell either of my girls they couldn't do something, and they'd about break their necks showing you that they not only could, but would. I'd have a chat with Hank when things settled down and see if I could get him to back off, assuming he did hold Cousin Will Ann's foolish notion that the two kids shouldn't be dating.

I was washing down part of the donut with my coffee when Debby, Betty and Etta arrived.

"Our committee is meeting at Farley's Cafeteria for lunch so we can plan the Cruiser's next mystery tour. But we wanted to spend the morning with you first," Debby informed me.

"Thank you all for coming. We can use all the prayers we get."

I asked Cousin Hank to lead us in prayer, partly for Jack's safe recovery and partly to say grace over the donuts. Then the new arrivals eagerly pounced on the half-full box.

The rest of our waiting time was spent munching and chatting, with the car club gals working to keep my mind off Jack's situation as much as they could by asking me to suggest different locations for our next mystery tour. I loved mystery tours because we always took off early on a Saturday morning, driving in formation down the highway, with only the leader knowing where we'd eventually wind up. The committee always chose really neat places that Jack and I had promised we'd visit but hadn't seemed to find the time for on our own.

I'd never realized how much these waiting room visits helped families pass the time while a loved one had surgery. And I supposed it helped to have the support there, if—heaven forbid—the news was bad. Please, God, let it not be bad news for Jack.

I refilled my cup from the waiting room pot that looked like it had been brewed sometime last month and sat down. Dr. Morrison strode into the waiting room, calling for the Bloodworth family. I almost didn't recognize him in the ugly, pea-green scrubs.

I jumped up, knocking my cup over and spilling coffee on the magazines beneath. I dusted the stray drops off my slacks and grabbed my walker, rolling over to meet him.

"Mrs. Bloodworth." He shook hands all around as I introduced my daughters. "Mr. Bloodworth came through the surgery just fine. No problems at all. I cut the tumor out, along with quite a bit of the tissue surrounding it, to make sure I got it all."

Dr. Morrison's surgical mask dangled over his chest, with one tie still caught behind his ear. It was all I could do not to reach up and pull it free. I am, and always have been, a neat freak, particularly when upset. I forced myself to concentrate. This sounded almost like good news.

"What about his lymph glands?" Sunny asked.

I nodded, too numb to come up with any sensible questions of my own. Jack had made it through the surgery. That was all that mattered for the moment. Well, almost all.

"I took a few of those out, as well, to send off for the biopsy. I'll have the report in about a week. We'll know more then."

"But couldn't you tell by looking, whether or not it's c-a-n-c-e-r?" Maggie spelled out the end of her question to prevent bigger questions from those with little ears who stood on either side of her, ever watchful.

"No, ma'am, I couldn't. Sometimes I can." He glanced down at the children. "If it's spread," he whispered. "This one was still encapsulated, and that's good news, even if it is cancer."

He turned to me. "I know this is hard for you and Mr. Bloodworth, so I'll get the results to you as quickly as I can. Then we'll know what further treatment, if any, is necessary. I'll have the nurse make Mr. Bloodworth an appointment with my office before you leave here today. You can take him home when he wakes up and knows for sure where he is."

Dr. Morrison pulled the mask completely off, leaned over, and winked at me. "And no hanky-panky until the stitches come out and the soreness goes away, okay?"

I blushed and nodded. Maggie choked, and I could swear Sunny giggled, but if she did, she hid it well.

"Ah, donuts. I missed breakfast." Dr. Morrison grabbed a napkin, snatched the last caramel-covered donut out of the box, and headed toward the waiting room door.

"Great news, Cousin Kitty. Now, if you'll excuse me, I've got to get to work. Busy day ahead," Hank said. "Two prospective clients are looking at my used cars, and I've got a shipment of new ones due in on a transport truck."

"Thanks for finding me a replacement van so quickly, Cousin Hank," Maggie said. "I really like it."

"No problem. And I've got my eye out for a good, used Volkswagen for you, Cousin Kitty. I know how much you loved your old bug."

"Thanks, Cousin Hank. I really do appreciate that, though I don't know when I'll be able to drive again. But when I do, much as I miss Beetle, I'll need something bigger and heavier." In case I ever found myself trapped again, so I'd have more room to move around.

"And thanks for coming to sit with us today," I said. "It means a lot. I'll tell Jack you were here. I know he'll appreciate it."

"Most welcome," he said, and waved as he headed for the waiting room door.

Craig busied himself gathering up the used cups and wadded napkins, stuffing them into the empty donut box, and dumping it into the large trash can near the door.

"I've got a class in an hour, Cousin Kitty," he said. "I'll call later to see how Cousin Jack's feeling." He turned for a final glance at Sunny as he pushed through the door.

Etta headed for the bathroom, and the rest of us took our seats again, with small sighs of relief.

Debby took my hand. "We'll sit with you until Jack wakes up and you can see him."

I nodded my thanks.

Maggie wondered out-loud why on earth the doctor would mention s-e-x in regard to people our age. Sunny collapsed in an all-out spasm of laughter, and Debby grinned while I wondered if Maggie was too old to spank. I probably didn't have the strength for it. Not today. Jack had made it through the surgery just fine. But what would the biopsy show? If it was cancer, could he survive chemo? Or would he just give up and die?

And could we possibly somehow get really lucky and have the tests show it not to be cancer at all? It was going to be a very long week.

CHAPTER TWENTY-FIVE

Two days after Jack's surgery, Detective Parker paid us a visit. I seated him in the living room. The sun porch was for family and friends.

"Lovely farm you have here. I see you put out several acres of corn. Didn't you say you were retired?" His over-sized frame slid slowly into Jack's favorite over-stuffed chair. The ancient ceiling fan lazily stirred the cool evening air around us.

Jack took a seat on the couch beside me and reached for my hand. I wasn't fooled. He wasn't trying to comfort me so much as he was trying to keep me quiet.

"I am retired," he said. "Friend of ours rents the land from me. Between the rent and Social Security, we get by."

Parker leaned back in the chair as if he had all day to chat, and my patience ran out. "Have you found out anything about Cousin Will Ann's killer yet?"

He shook his head mournfully.

"Honey, why don't you make us some coffee?" Jack said. "I sure could use a cup. How about you, Detective?"

"Well, I wouldn't want to be any trouble." Parker nodded toward my walker.

I could've smacked Jack and probably would've if Parker hadn't been sitting there. Jack was trying to slow me down, or get rid of me so he could talk to Parker alone. Nice try, but I'd spent a lot of years in that old kitchen, and I could hear and talk as easily from there as I could from the couch. I grabbed my walker and scooted my way across the living room floor.

"Is there any news about Will Ann's case?" Jack asked as I filled the pot with water.

It took me several seconds to wrestle loose a filter, blowing and rubbing until I'd managed to separate one filter from the others. I was trying to see what was going on over the breakfast bar while I measured the grounds into the pot. Of course Parker mumbled his answer so I couldn't hear. I had never allowed my students to mumble in class. I wondered where my ruler was. Good thing I'd misplaced it. Detective Parker would probably arrest me for assault if I found it.

Jack and Parker continued to talk in low tones. Jack Bloodworth was going to hear about that from me when Parker left.

"Coffee's ready," I announced, and Jack limped over to carry the tray for me. Weren't we a fine pair, two birds with broken wings?

I started to send just coffee into the living room with him, but my conscience wouldn't allow me to leave the other end of the tray empty, so I fished the rest of the carrot cake out of the pantry. Shame to waste it on Detective Parker, but my mother had taught me proper company manners, and even after nearly sixty years, her voice in my head was hard to ignore.

When we were seated and Parker was scooping up his cake, he began to ask questions. "And you still don't remember anything about your accident?" he asked.

"The last thing I remember is going to Wal-Mart over in Paducah with Maggie." Still using company manners, I left out the part about Billy throwing up in the shopping cart. "I needed cleaning supplies and Maggie was grocery shopping. According to my daughter that was several days before Cousin Will Ann's murder. After that," I shrugged, "nothing."

"Not even finding the body? That was pretty difficult for you," Parker said.

"Which is one of the reasons the doctor said I couldn't remember."

"Did the doctor say why you can't remember the accident?"

Detective Parker leaned forward and placed his now-empty plate on the tray, glancing at it pointedly. I didn't offer him seconds. If his mother hadn't taught him company manners, that was his problem. Besides, I wasn't about to shuffle back into the kitchen and cut another piece. I had a few questions of my own.

Ignoring his question, I said, "I remember waking up when Jack found me and I remember the firemen beginning to cut me out of my car. Next thing I knew I was in the emergency room in a whole lot of pain. Everything in between Wal-Mart and Lourdes Hospital is pretty much a blur. Now," I demanded, "what have you learned about Cousin Will Ann's murder?"

I bumped my good ankle against Jack's good ankle to let him know to keep quiet. It was time for some answers.

Detective Parker set his cup down and looked me straight in the eye. I had a feeling that whatever was coming wasn't good, so I set my cup down as well and reached for Jack's hand.

"Your accident happened on the Kentucky side of the Brookport Bridge," Parker said, "so our officers were called in to investigate it. The accident re-constructionist did a thorough job, which included examining your daughter's stolen van. Since it was parked so near to where you were found, we figured it had to be involved."

I snorted. Parker wasn't the only one who knew how to detect. "We already figured out why Maggie's van was there, Detective. It was stolen sometime around eleven or eleven-thirty, just about the time I usually leave aerobics. I had on my exercise outfit when they found me, and my friends said I had been at aerobics that morning. Obviously, I saw someone driving Maggie's van and followed them. Since I didn't have a cell phone—" I cut my gaze toward Jack, not wanting to stir up fresh guilt. He grinned at me, so I continued. "I must have followed the thief so I could report where Maggie's van was. Unfortunately, I had the accident."

"And it doesn't strike you as odd that the thief had an accident just a hundred or so yards further down the road?" Parker gave me that one-up-on-you grin I hated.

I gave him one right back. "I must've gotten too close and hit Maggie's van. Then I went off the road. That would've caused the other driver to wreck as well." I squared my shoulders.

"Mrs. Bloodworth," Parker began.

"Kitty. Please. Mrs. Bloodworth was Jack's mother," I said, before I gave it enough thought.

Great. Now Parker and I would be on a first name basis.

"Horace." Parker nodded in our direction.

I coughed. Horace? I thought all detectives had tough-guy first names like Ridge or Rance or Rob or something.

"Kitty, I'm afraid I have some bad news. That's why I came here in person today. According to the accident reconstructionist, Mrs. Jamison's van hit your car, not the other way around . . ." He paused to let that sink in.

I felt my blood pressure drop. "But that can't be, why would . . ." I ran out of steam.

Jack scratched his chin. "That makes sense," he said. "But who was driving the van? You can't possibly think it was Maggie?"

"No, I don't think it was your daughter, but I did question her about it."

Jack squeezed my hand hard before I could take umbrage at that statement.

"Mrs. Jamison was at home that day, after eleven-thirty. We've spoken to one neighbor who saw her hanging out clothes on the line just shortly after, and another whose children visited hers.

She was there, all right." Parker picked up his coffee cup.

Jack refilled his and mine from the thermos and handed me my cup. I took it numbly.

"Then who was driving her van?" Jack asked. "Have you found out by fingerprints or anything?"

I think I knew the answer before Parker gave it.

"We found lots of prints belonging to your daughter and her family, not to mention plenty of other things."

With two children riding in that vehicle, I deemed it best not to ask what those other things were.

"But nothing at all from the thief," Parker continued, "so he or she must've worn gloves. No hair or fibers either, I'm sorry to say."

No sorrier than I was to hear it.

I found my voice at last. "But how can you be so sure the van hit me instead of the other way around?"

"Because the damage to the van was confined to the front bumper and hood. The damage to your vehicle, of course, was all over. If you'd hit the van while following it, the damage would have been to the van's rear. Therefore, the van was following you, not, as you thought, the other way around."

As Parker let that sink in, I felt like sinking through the floor.

"I must say, Kitty, you have a great deal of courage to have survived that accident. Particularly since you were trapped in the wreckage for so many hours. You're very lucky to be alive."

I nodded. I'd been thanking the Good Lord daily for that one ever since I'd woken up in the emergency room.

I screwed up my courage and asked the question I dreaded but had to. "Isn't it possible that I had just passed the other driver, trying to cut him off?" I ducked my head, not daring to look into Jack's eyes. "I might have done that if I was mad enough."

"No," came from Parker and Jack at the same time. Parker

let Jack finish.

"Kitty, you went off the road right past the guard rail, in the curve that slopes downward. There is no way you would have ever tried to pass anyone in that curve, mad or not."

Parker nodded. "From the scratches on your bumper, it looks like the driver hit you at an angle on purpose, in order to fishtail you over to the shoulder and off the edge. That took some skill."

"Skill I certainly don't have. And I wouldn't have hit Maggie's van on purpose, no matter how mad I was. She adored it. So did the kids."

Jack looked at Parker. "So what's the bottom line here, Horace?"

I swallowed a giggle.

Parker said, "The bottom line is, someone deliberately ran Kitty off the road. Tried to kill her, and they very nearly succeeded. That's a mighty powerful coincidence. So either someone is after your family, or someone thinks you know something." He looked at me. "And that someone is bound to try again."

Chapter Twenty-Six

After Parker left, Jack and I went out to the sun porch. We intended to sit down and relax. Instead, the mid-morning sunshine called us outside. Thankfully, there was a large bare spot just beyond the porch. It had been worn down by the girls and their friends playing there over the years and the lack of sun due to the big old shade tree behind the garage. I'd insisted on filling that area in with flat rocks several years ago to create a patio, and now it provided me with a reasonably level area to roll my walker across. The crutches had allowed me to move much faster. And I hated the walker, wheels not withstanding, but it forced me to put all my weight on my legs, and, according to my hulky therapist, I'd walk unaided much faster by practicing now with the walker. That was the only reasoning that induced me to stick with the hateful thing.

We stood on the stone patio and watched the clouds scroll by overhead, putting on their usual lovely show. Clouds in Southern Illinois were generally spectacular, with shapes, sizes and shades that defied description. Today's display was no exception.

A turkey vulture glided overhead, swooping this way and that, dropping lower and lower with each pass. Ugly birds, they were enough to scare the life out of any prey, except they liked to feed on things that were already dead.

"That turkey vulture reminds me of Detective Parker," I said. "Circling around, hoping to pounce on someone."

"Truth is, Parker did us a big favor today, by filling us in on your accident. Now we know to be on our guard. And you go nowhere without me, until he arrests Will Ann's killer. Got that?" Jack ordered.

It was all I could do not to shout "Sir, yes sir!" and salute, but I wasn't going to give my darling husband the satisfaction. I had to admit, Parker had definitely made me shake in my socks. Someone had tried to kill me. Why? Because they hated me? Because they thought I knew something? Maybe because I did know something, only now I couldn't remember but might later on. No matter which reason prevailed, it wasn't comforting to know I'd been run off the road and left to die.

Speaking of the dead, the large vulture suddenly disappeared behind the pole barn, and I felt afraid. Did it know there had been a body inside the pole barn not long ago? Worse thought, was there another dead body nearby now?

Jack must've been thinking the same thing. "Stay here," he ordered, "I'll see what that bird is after. You might get your wheels stuck in the dirt by the barn."

I knew he was more afraid that there might be another body nearby, and he didn't want me to go through that experience again. Vultures rarely landed on the ground without the promise of dinner.

I leaned on the walker, shivering in the sunshine. Finally, growing tired of standing in one position, I made my way slowly back onto the porch. It would be much warmer in there, out of the breeze, and I could rest my bones, particularly the ones that were still healing.

Jack finally returned to our back yard, glancing around for me.

"In here, on the porch."

He shaded his eyes and, spotting me at last, came inside.

"What was it?"

"One of John's calves. Looked like a newborn. Must've gotten separated from its momma and the coyotes killed it. Mr. Turkey Vulture was finishing off what the other varmints left."

"Does John know? He can't afford to lose many more calves after the tough year he's had."

"Yeah, he was out there when I went behind the barn. The calf was on his side of the fence."

That figured. Jack never could meet up with our neighbor, John Holmes, without chatting for a month straight. They'd known each other for decades. You'd think they'd have run out of conversation by now. John never married nor had kids. His herd was his whole life. I often fixed extra for dinner and sent part to him because he'd get busy with his animals and forget to eat. At least I'd done that before my accident. If John was counting on me since then, he was in serious danger of starvation.

I glanced at Jack and noticed he was staring at the pole barn.

"What's wrong?"

"Nothing."

"Nothing, schmothing, I know that look. What's bothering you, Jack Bloodworth?"

"John asked how we were both doing, you since the accident, and me since the surgery. I said 'fine.' Then he said something about how lucky we were to have Craig around, helping out the last few weeks."

"We are lucky to have him. I don't know how we'd have gotten by if he hadn't done the weekly mowing for you since this all started. Joe's working too much overtime right now to do it." I didn't mention that mowing the five acres surrounding our house, in the heat of summer, was getting to be a bit much for Jack. We'd had that conversation before. Many times.

"That's what I thought he meant, but John apologized for not realizing we needed help before your accident. He said he saw Craig out at the pole barn carrying something to his car.

He brought it back later."

Jack turned to me. "If John's right, it was before your accident and before Will Ann's murder. I hadn't given Craig the key to my barn then. So how did he get into the pole barn? And what did he take without telling me?"

"When, exactly, was this?" Maybe Jack had misunderstood, or John Holmes had gotten his dates mixed up?

"Two days before Will Ann's murder. John remembers because he had six cows near to calving, and the first one delivered that day. He marks the dates down on that big ugly calendar in his kitchen. The calf survived, but that's why John was so close to our pole barn. The last calf was born today. The one that didn't make it."

Might as well put it into words since we were both thinking it. "So how did Craig get into the barn?"

"Yeah, since I have the only key."

I stopped myself in mid-nod. "The girls have keys. Don't you remember? You gave each of them one when we went on vacation to the Grand Canyon with the car club three years ago. Maggie lost hers while we were still out west. Tori flushed it down the toilet. But Sunny likely still has hers. Maybe she gave it to him."

Which wasn't good. If Craig killed his mother and hid her in our trunk, Sunny would have to be involved, whether she meant to be or not, unless he'd stolen the key from her. We'd have to call her over for a talk. And she wasn't going to like it. But she couldn't keep protecting Craig if he was guilty, no matter how close they were. And just exactly how close were they?

CHAPTER TWENTY-SEVEN

After a fairly sleepless night, Jack drove me over to Paducah for my therapy. During the long weeks he'd been bringing me across the river for my daily work-outs with my physical therapist, the car club Romeos, bless their hearts, had been driving all the way over there as well to meet Jack for breakfast.

I still wasn't able to do aerobics, but I missed the girls, so on the way home I had Jack drop me off at the Senior Center. I knew someone would taxi me back home later.

The girls greeted me with the usual flurry of hugs. While they "Sweated to the Oldies," I sat on the floor on my mat in what wasn't even close to a yoga position and relaxed my breathing. Parker had said someone tried to kill me. Somehow I couldn't wrap my brain around that. Kill Cousin Will Ann, yes, kill me, no, because no one ever wants to accept the idea that anyone else would put them permanently out of the way. So what was going on? Did the killer hate everyone in our family? Just the women? Or did the killer think I knew something?

Maybe I should call Arden's and have a silly T-shirt printed that said something like: I NEED A MEMORY TRANS-PLANT. Karen Arden had done a terrific job on our family reunion T-shirts a couple of years back. Cousin Will Ann refused to wear hers, showing up in a silk dress, so of course she stood out like a white beacon amongst all the red shirts printed with: HALLIBURTON FAMILY — WE LIVE TO EAT on the front and a cute little pig on the back. Halliburton family members were nothing if not honest.

I gently switched legs to cross one over the other and took deep breaths. Etta Strong was sweating like a parson caught in a cat house, and I was a little afraid she'd have a heart attack. Apparently common sense kicked in because she stopped struggling through the moves and came over and plopped down beside me.

"How's it going?" she gasped.

"Fine," I lied. "Therapy is getting easier every day."

Actually it was getting harder, but I wasn't one to whine. Well, not unless I thought it would get Jack off the couch and washing the dishes. And, mentally, I was still worrying over everything that'd happened.

"Happy to hear it. You've gotta strengthen those old bones. Don't want to be on that walker forever, do you?"

"Actually, the therapist said I can graduate to a cane today. I thought maybe after lunch, you, and Debby—and whoever else wants to go—could run me over to Paducah to check out the antique stores. I'd have Jack take me, but those stores bore him silly. He'd much rather be puttering in the pole barn."

"Wonderful," Etta said. "We could have lunch at Kirchhoff's Bakery. I adore their chicken salad."

My mouth watered. Their bread was wonderful as well. Maybe I'd bring some home to Jack.

At last Shirley Mumfort turned the music off, rolled out her yoga mat, and began cooling the girls down. I did the upper body stretches with them, thanking the Good Lord I could now breathe without pain. My lung had healed and the infection was gone.

The rest of the girls had places to go and people to see, or so they said, so Etta, Debby, and I headed to Paducah in Debby's '63 Mustang. I loved riding in that car.

I called Jack on my cell phone to let him know where we'd

be. He wasn't crazy about me taking a trip back across the river without him, but I assured him I'd be fine with the girls along. He made me promise to check in when we arrived there, and when we started home. I reluctantly agreed and hung up.

Etta glanced nervously at me as we neared the old blue bridge. "Are you really sure about this, Kitty?"

I'd told Debby to take us to Paducah via the Brookport Bridge rather than the more modern, four lane I-24 bridge. And I'd carefully neglected to mention that fact to Jack.

"I have to face it sometime, Etta. Besides, it's much closer to downtown Paducah this way."

Debby slowed way down for the thirty-mile-per-hour speed limit through the small nearby town of Brookport, Illinois. No use getting a ticket. But she hit the metal deck of the bridge and tromped the gas petal, eager, as usual, to get across the old narrow bridge and onto the other side. I was riding shotgun and I gripped the arm rest on the door with both hands and prayed. The Ohio River was as smooth as glass today, an unusual sight. Generally the wind kept it pretty well white-capped. I watched the tow boats lining up to lock through on the Illinois side. A muscle boat zipped underneath the bridge and up the river, and I turned to watch it come out from under the other side.

"Lovely day to be on the river," Etta observed from the back seat of the Mustang. "I always feel sorry for the deck hands when it's cold and rainy. Big chance one of them might slip and fall over the side and . . ." she trailed off.

Deb braked the car to a near-crawl as we reached the end of the bridge. "Do you want me to pull over?" she asked.

"If you can do it safely," I said, still gripping the arm rest. "Jack refuses to even drive over this bridge, much less stop for me to see where the accident happened. But I know I have to face it sooner or later."

Deb eased over onto the shoulder of the road, parked, and turned off the engine. I opened the door, pulled myself up out of the butter-soft seat, and leaned against the window frame. Deb came around to my side of the car and put her arm around me. Etta leaned over the front seat and peered out.

Yellow crime scene tape still tied around several bushes below us flapped gently in the breeze. There were deep gouges where my bug had bounced end-over-end down the hill. I shed a tear for my little VW, but my next vehicle would definitely be something far more substantial, like Etta's awkward old 1939 Ford. Some sort of hulking piece of machinery that wouldn't roll head-first over anything unless the entire world suddenly tilted sharply on its axis.

I felt more tears running down my cheeks. I had taken a pretty bad beating because of the accident and the person who'd caused it, but I'd survived, and I was overcoming the problems it left behind, bit by bit, day by day. Someone wanted me dead, but he or she had failed, and I was on the alert now. So were the police, not to mention my friends and family. I was no longer afraid or sad. I was mad. Killing me now, for whatever reason, was going to take a lot of guts and a lot of thought, and I planned to be much gutsier and thoughtier.

Whoever you are, you missed your chance. From now on, I'll be ready.

Kirchhoff's, as always, smelled like heaven. I added potato salad to my usual order of chicken salad on a croissant and those wonderful grapes dipped in sugar. I might be near-comatose by the time we headed back to Metropolis, but I'd be happy.

We took a seat at a wobbly wrought-iron table, and I glanced around, as I always did, at the marvelous pictures on the wall of the original bakery when it was in operation early in the last century. The huge skylight flooded the room with warmth. We each ate in respectful silence, enjoying the food and watching the other down-towners having lunch and discussing private things, as if the rest of the eaters couldn't overhear.

The guy at the next table had just given his credit card number and password to someone on the other end of his cell phone, evidently in order to ask a question about a payment he'd recently made. And victims always wondered how identity theft happened to them. I'd received a document shredder for Christmas from Maggie, and I only gave out private information on the non-cordless phone at home, in a whisper. Debby grinned at me when the guy finally hung up and turned to his lunch, and Etta gave him a look that should have frozen him to his chair. He didn't appear to notice.

The first two antique shops produced nothing in the way of usable canes, but Etta bought a hat to add to the collection hanging on her bedroom wall, and a fox stole that made me drool. But, according to Debby, one doesn't snatch the really good finds out of a friend's hands. One waits and hopes said friend sets it down, and then one snatches and runs for the cash register. Etta was far too experienced to let that happen.

Debby bought a set of Beaded Block dessert plates that matched her growing Depression glass collection. "I promise, I'll serve you gals cake on these right after the next car club officers' meeting at my house."

"Walnut cake?" Etta inquired, to which Debby nodded. I clutched my chest. Debby's walnut cake was moist and delicious, and her secret as closely guarded as anything Uncle Sam had ever stored at the Pentagon. I hoped the next meeting was scheduled real soon.

I got lucky at the third antique store. A stout wooden cane, hand-carved with Dogwood blossoms, stood nearly hidden in a corner beside a jelly cabinet. It had a rubber stopper on the bottom to keep the owner from sliding and possibly re-injuring a leg or two. I picked the cane up and looked it over. Underneath the flat handle was carved the words "To My Beloved Jewel, from Joseph." And below that, the date, November 20, 1904. I showed it to Debby—Etta was now engrossed in reading a first edition Bobbsey Twins she'd found in a basket—and Debby wondered aloud if Jewel was a nickname or the woman's real name.

"Jewel was a popular name for girls in the early nineteen hundreds," I said. "It was my great aunt's name as well."

Debby always wondered about the former owners of her treasures. Now she had me wondering. The cane couldn't possibly have belonged to my great aunt, could it? But her husband had been named Joseph, as well, certainly a very large coincidence. Well, whoever Jewel was, she had been much loved by Joseph. And she'd taken great care of this wonderful hand-carved piece of useful artwork.

I checked the price and swallowed hard. A hundred bucks. Jack Bloodworth would have a stroke. Well, he'd just have to get over it. I wasn't leaving this beautiful thing here in a dark, dusty corner with no one to enjoy it.

I hobbled my way to the front desk, pushing my walker with the cane hung over the top, just before we discovered that Debby's car had been broken into and my purse stolen. What a dope I'd been to leave it in her car.

CHAPTER TWENTY-EIGHT

Fortunately Debby had worn her fanny pack that morning, with her money, credit cards, and the all-important cell phone inside. I, on the other hand, had tucked my purse under a blanket in the back seat because it was difficult to push the walker and manage my purse at the same time. Moving from store to store, I thought it would be easier to leave it behind. I'd have kicked myself, but couldn't manage it with the walker. Debby dialed 9-1-1 and reported the theft, then charged my cane on her card so I could pay her back later. What would we do without friends?

While we waited for the police to arrive I made a quick decision about how to handle the most immediate problem. Canceling my credit cards. Like most Internet users, I'd seen friends inundate other friends with e-mails about how to protect oneself from credit card theft, and what to do if those measures didn't work.

Several months ago I'd taken everything out of my wallet and photocopied the important items on my little printer at home, then carefully tucked that information into my desk. I could easily call Jack and have him read the necessary numbers over the phone to me. At which point he would likely hang up on me and dash over to Paducah to see for himself that I was okay, despite any assurances I might give him over the phone.

Okay, how could I get around him and still get the information? Sunny was in Carbondale, spending the day at the library researching a term paper. Maggie's kids were probably napping, but I was getting desperate. I made the call using Debby's cell phone. After several seconds of squawking like a frantic mother hen, Maggie understood my dilemma and agreed to go out to our house, find the information filed away in my desk, and call me back with it when she got home.

She also agreed to simply tell her father that I needed some phone numbers that weren't in my cell phone yet, which was the truth. She was not to mention that I was no longer in possession of said cell phone. Not unless he specifically asked.

The bowling ball I'd been living with since Jack's illness dropped from somewhere around my throat, straight into my stomach again. I'd lost my precious new cell phone. And after years of angling to get Jack to sign up for the service. My "free" phone was about to cost me several hundred dollars, and I seriously doubted Jack had thought to take out the insurance the cell phone company offered. He'd always refused to buy that kind of insurance on any appliance we bought. I sighed. This was really bad. The credit cards could be easily cancelled but the phone was going to be costly. And Jack was going to be cranky.

Why hadn't I thought to wear my fanny pack like Debby? I knew I couldn't wag that heavy purse around, but I'd grabbed it up this morning by habit. And I hadn't really planned to go shopping for a cane until my therapist told me I could move up from the walker. So I'd left my purse in Debby's car instead of asking one of the girls to carry it for me. I didn't think anyone would break the car window and snatch it. Not when she'd parked on a busy side street in downtown Paducah.

Of course, I hadn't thought anyone would put a dead body in the trunk of our car when it was safely locked up in the pole barn either. Well, I obviously wasn't any more identity-theft-savvy than the cell phone guy at Kirchhoff's. It was indeed difficult to teach an old dog new tricks.

Maggie called me back, and, using Debby's cell phone again, I got to work informing the credit card companies that our accounts needed to be shut down immediately. Thankfully we only had three cards, the main one Jack and I used for gas, groceries, or anything else we bought, and two cards issued by local chain stores that I hadn't used since before the accident. Those were paid off, and the card we used routinely wouldn't have much on it this early in the month, so we should be okay in that respect.

"Why don't you call your cell phone company as well?" Debby suggested. "They can track any calls made on your phone and maybe even locate the thief. If it's kids, most likely they will use it right away."

"Great idea."

I was in the middle of that call when Horace Parker lumbered in, banging open the heavy antique door of the shop. "I was having a late lunch at my desk when Mrs. Evans' call came through." He looked at Debby like he thought she'd personally arranged to have my purse stolen just to interrupt his lunch. "Dispatch alerted me because your name is tied to the Lloyd murder case. What happened?"

Now he was glaring at me, but Deb filled him in while I finished explaining that I couldn't give the cell phone company employee my new number because I'd not yet memorized it and the phone was now gone so I couldn't look it up. The person on the other end—for whom English was a third or possibly fourth language that obviously hadn't been mastered as of yet—struggled to understand every single word I said. Ditto for me understanding him.

Parker yanked the phone out of my hand, gave his badge number to the cell phone company employee, and shouted orders for him to look up my account and track any calls coming from my number. The employee's ability to comprehend the

English language apparently underwent a sudden transformation for the better, and Parker snapped the little phone shut and handed it back to me. I passed it to Debby and waited for Parker's questions.

Debby and I had taken seats on a fifties style sofa in the antique shop where I'd bought my cane. She'd collapsed my walker and left it in her trunk. I found myself wishing the perps, as Parker referred to them, would come back and steal the walker. Of course, I could always donate it to the Senior Center. I was quickly ashamed to remember that there were folks there who would be thankful to have it.

"So, Kitty, someone swiped your purse? Any reason to think this might be tied to Mrs. Lloyd's murder or your accident?"

Deb raised an eyebrow at me when Parker called me by my first name, but it seemed to pass right over Etta's head. In fact, she'd snuggled into a nearby rocker, and I could almost swear she was snoring.

"Of course not," I said. "Why would the killer want my credit cards or cell phone?"

"Maybe you had something else in your purse that the killer wanted?" Parker eased into a nearby chair with a large sign tacked to the back that said: PLEASE DO NOT SIT IN THIS CHAIR, IT'S VERY OLD.

Out of the corner of my eye I saw the owner of the antique store sit down rather quickly behind the counter and put her head in her hands.

I opened my mouth to assure Parker that there was absolutely nothing in my purse a thief would want, aside from credit cards and the cell phone, but quickly closed my mouth again.

True, I rarely carried cash. My teacher's retirement check and Jack's Social Security went into our account by direct deposit, and I hated driving to the bank to cash a check. Most of the time we simply used that one main credit card for everything we purchased, then Jack wrote a check at the end of the month to cover it, with no interest due. So while I really hadn't cleaned out my purse since some time before the accident, I couldn't imagine anything in there being valuable enough to steal.

"Someone deliberately ran you off the road, Kitty. We have to assume that either an unknown person or persons has a grudge against your family or someone thinks you know something about Mrs. Lloyd's murder and wants to eliminate you. Women carry a lot of important information in their purses. My wife's could hold every single file in the Paducah Police Department, with room left over. What was in yours that a killer might want?"

"I honestly don't know, Horace."

Debby choked. Whether it was over my use of Parker's first name or the idea of his being married, I couldn't say. I shot her a warning glance and 'fessed up to not having cleaned out my purse since I couldn't remember when.

Parker shook his head. I wondered how long it had been since he'd cleaned out his wallet, but I didn't dare ask.

"I have officers checking the dumpsters in the area," Parker said. "If the thief is male, and on foot, he won't want to be seen carrying a purse. Give me a description of it so I can call it in."

I gave the best description I could, and had to hold myself in my seat when Parker snickered over the "blue gingham" part. So what did his lovely wife carry, a Dooney and Bourke? No, probably a knock-off.

All at once I started to cry. Parker assumed the typical horrified male expression, and Debby put her arm around my shoulder. Etta woke up with a snort, fluffed her crushed curls, and asked, "What's going on?"

I honked into the tissue Debby thoughtfully provided. Then I swallowed. How in the world did Debby manage to get so much into that small fanny pack? As soon as I got home, I'd get mine out, despite the fact that I had absolutely nothing at present to carry in it. That brought fresh tears to my eyes, and Parker out of his seat to ask the store owner for a glass of water. I was touched until he downed the glass himself and plopped back into the chair, ignoring the owner's murmured protests. The chair squeaked, and I wondered if Parker was about to take home a very expensive "as is."

"I'm sorry," I said to no one in particular. "It just brought back the fact that I can't remember a single thing since right before Cousin Will Ann's murder. If I did know anything that would lead to her killer, I certainly can't call it up now. And it never occurred to me to look through my purse after the accident. So if I did have anything important in there, it's gone."

I sobbed into the tissue again, and Debby spoke to Parker in a tight voice. "Can't you see how difficult this is for Kitty? She's doing the best she can."

Parker had the grace to look abashed when I peeked over the tissue at him. Time to stop hiding behind it and come back into the discussion.

"I'm fine," I said. "I didn't mean to lose it like that. I thought I was doing better."

"You are much better," Debby comforted. "But there are bound to be steps backward every now and then, for all the steps forward."

I knew she was right. Time to stop beating up on myself.

"I'll tell Jack about this when I get home and have him and the girls go over whatever they remember about my activities between the day of the murder and my accident. Maybe we can figure out something from that."

Parker nodded. Obviously that hadn't occurred to him. Well, it hadn't occurred to me either, so no harm, no foul.

The store owner handed me a cup of water, and as I took a sip the front door banged open again and the bell announced a uniformed police officer with my blue gingham purse slung carelessly over his shoulder. Obviously, the tall, dark-haired young man was totally secure in his masculinity.

"Found this about a half a block from the victim's car," he announced to Parker.

"Thanks." Parker took the purse, winked at me, and dumped the contents out on the antique tray table between us. Thankfully, the table had a glass top. Otherwise, the keys alone would have done several hundred dollars worth of damage that I had no intention of paying for.

I took a deep breath. Keys meant the thief couldn't get into our house, unless he'd had time to get copies made, which I doubted, because the nearest place with that capability was way the other side of Paducah. My beloved cell phone slid out of the front zippered pocket when Parker opened it, and I breathed another sigh of relief, until I realized I had to call the company back and probably explain to the self-same employee that they no longer needed to block my service or trace the calls.

My wallet, along with my driver's license and credit cards, were all gone. I was thankful I'd cancelled the cards. Parker went through every single item in my purse, one by one, putting each under close inspection while I squirmed. A half-eaten snack bar was still stuffed inside a plastic baggie along with an empty water bottle. Obviously my purse had been in worse need of a clean-out than I'd thought.

For a few seconds I was immensely relieved that the wad of little notes I usually wrote to myself and stuck into one particular pocket were gone. Much of my private life was generally jotted down in those notes, and they weren't meant to be read by nosy detectives. Then I realized that those notes most likely held the key to why I was going to Paducah the day I'd nearly died.

I would've cried again if I hadn't been determined not to be weak in front of Parker or to upset Debby and Etta again. But I did confess to him that the notes were missing and that I had no idea what I'd written beyond a very messy Wal-Mart list, probably a jot or two about upcoming dates, and possibly a wish list of things I was saving up to buy. Like a DVD player so I could collect some of those wonderful old scary movies from my childhood that were finally coming out on those neat little disks.

"You were saying?" Parker brought me back into the conversation.

"That's all I can think of that might be missing. Everything else seems to be there—comb, lipstick, paperback novel."

Parker looked at the novel in question, an Anne George Southern Sisters' mystery, and jotted down some notes on his ever-present little pad.

At last Parker stood and shook my hand, then nodded to the young officer. "Good work. Let's keep looking for Mrs. Bloodworth's wallet. And the sticky notes with her life history," he finished.

I gripped the cane, prepared to strike if he snickered, but he didn't so I relaxed.

"I'll be in touch, Kitty," he said. "Ladies." Parker very nearly bowed to Debby and Etta, before he swept out the door with the young officer bringing up the rear.

I thanked the store owner for letting us use her furniture for the interview, and we made our escape.

We drove home via I-24. I no longer needed to see the Brookport Bridge. I'd faced that ghost and I wasn't afraid of it any more, not even in light of today's unsetting developments. It was time to take back my life. And face Jack.

CHAPTER TWENTY-NINE

By the time Debby got me home, Jack was pacing the garage. In all the excitement I'd forgotten to call him.

"What happened?" he demanded. "And don't tell me 'nothing' because I'm not believing it."

"Something did happen. I'm going to tell you all about it, just as soon as I figure out how you knew. And I wouldn't mind sitting down to tell it."

We walked into the kitchen. I'd told Jack earlier, when he'd dropped me off at aerobics, that I'd heat up leftovers when I got home. He helped while we talked.

"So, how did you know something happened?"

"Maggie came by to pick up some caller information you didn't seem to have in your cell phone. She wouldn't look me in the eye. She's a lousy liar, just like her mother."

Like me? He was the one who looked at my chin whenever he didn't want to upset or alarm me. I let it pass.

"We were in an antique store and I found this wonderful cane." I held it up for him to inspect.

"Lovely, so what happened after you struck gold at the antique store?"

Jack was never one to allow a segue off the subject to intrude when he wanted to know something. Of course if it was me doing the asking, that was different.

I carefully spooned the leftovers onto two paper plates and placed Jack's in the microwave to heat.

"I was about to pay for the cane when I remembered I'd left my purse in Debby's car. It was covered up on the floorboard in the back seat, so I thought it would be safe."

"Uh huh, and?" Jack dropped ice from the freezer into our glasses.

"She came back all out of breath and said her car had been broken into. They smashed the window on the driver's side. My purse was gone."

He turned in the middle of pouring milk into his glass. I couldn't abide milk over ice, but Jack loved it and the colder the better. I always opted for water.

"Terrific. You probably didn't think about how Leo is going to kill Debby for this. He's a bit protective of that car."

I'd never met any antique car owners who weren't protective of their cars. With good reason, of course. But I actually had thought of that and promised Debby that we would pay to fix the window. I'd have to break that news to Jack as well.

"Anything else stolen or damaged?" Jack asked.

"Nope, just my purse."

The microwave dinged and Jack switched out the plates, setting his on the table. I appreciated not having to hobble to the counter again. I was suddenly very tired and sore. This hadn't been a good day to learn to use a cane instead of the walker.

"Anyhow, Debby came back and called the police on her cell phone—"

"Since yours was stolen, right? I told you that thing was worthless."

I held up my hand to stop the flood of protest that was about to hit the kitchen. "You're right, Jack. At that particular moment, I didn't have my cell phone. Anyhow, Parker showed up and asked all the right questions. While he was interviewing us about the theft, a young officer found my purse. The cell phone was still in it."

"Credit cards, too?"

"No, but I—"

"Great, now we'll owe everyone in the country. I never should have let—"

Whatever it was he shouldn't have let me do was lost in my explosion.

"Jack Bloodworth, I'm not a complete dummy, no matter what you think. Maggie gave me the numbers of the credit card companies—that's why I had her come out here—and I called and cancelled all of our cards. So don't try to charge anything until we get the new ones, or you'll wind up in jail, which might not be such a bad thing!"

He looked hurt as he pulled my plate out of the microwave. Maybe a bit of humor would defuse the situation.

"I just hope it was some teenage boy wanting to use my cards for a fake ID," I said. "I'd like to see him try to pass for a crippled old woman."

"You might be crippled for the moment, but you aren't old." Jack smiled and the tension eased.

"What did Parker think?" he asked.

Great, this was likely to make Jack mad all over again. But no way could I lie to him.

"He thinks it could be related to Cousin Will Ann's murder and my accident. At least he's keeping it in mind. He thinks maybe I had something in my purse that would've shed light on this mess. Like where I was going the day of the accident."

I took a bite of sweet potatoes. As usual, Jack had heated them for so long that I'd have to let them cool before I dared risk another bite. I took a quick gulp of water.

"I hate to say it, honey, but Parker could be right." Jack swallowed a bite that was bound to have burned all the way down his esophagus. "You live and die by your lists, just like that Frog or Toad character in the book you read to Tori every time she's here. You can't move if your list doesn't say it's time to go wherever it is you need to go."

I snorted. I was bad, but not quite that bad. Well, maybe a little.

"The lists I keep were missing, Jack. I could kick myself for that, but neither of my legs will reach that high at the moment. I should've cleaned out my purse as soon as I got home from the hospital, but I just didn't feel like fooling with it. Too much else on my mind, I guess."

He leaned over to my side of the table and squeezed my hand. "You've been through a lot. Don't worry about it. If the thief was Will Ann's killer and he or she got something important out of your purse, maybe that will make you safe. No reason to come after you if you don't have the information."

I tried another bite of sweet potatoes. They were just right.

"Maybe." I put my fork down. "I want you to know something else. Debby, Etta, and I stopped at the edge of the Brookport Bridge on our way to Paducah. The spot where the accident happened."

Jack's eyebrows went up.

"I needed to go there again if I was ever going to be able to put this all behind me. I've made a decision not to let this get me down. I do have physical limitations that I'll have to live with for quite a while, because of the accident, but I'm not going to let myself live in fear. Like you said the other night, we have to get on with our lives."

"But you do have to be very careful, Kitty. Just because your purse was the only thing taken this time doesn't mean Will Ann's killer has given up on getting at you. From now on, I go where you go."

I opened my mouth, but Jack didn't give me a chance to protest.

"I mean what I say, woman. Until this case is solved, you and

I will be joined at your good hip."

I narrowed my eyes at him. "I bet any amount of money that I could get rid of you, if I really wanted to. I'll just make sure the girls and I eat at a restaurant you hate, and there are a multitude of those, starting with Chinese and ending with Italian. Or that we go shopping at the mall. You wouldn't last fifteen minutes."

He reached over and shook my hand. "That's a bet, Little Missy. Better sign over your next retirement check to me. You won't be needing it."

Yeah? We'd see.

CHAPTER THIRTY

After dinner we sat on the back porch in the dark. The last of the fireflies for this season were making a valiant effort to light up our back yard. I've always loved watching them dart up and down, blinking off and on like a crazed string of miniature Christmas lights. For once I was glad the security light had burned out and Jack hadn't gotten around to replacing the bulb.

An owl in the tree just behind the pole barn kept challenging all the nearby night creatures to give him their identities.

We'd been enjoying the evening sounds for about thirty minutes when a figure stepped out from behind the pole barn.

Jack leaped up and was headed inside for his shotgun when I stopped him. "Wait, it's just John Holmes."

Jack dropped into the seat beside me again and muttered, "John should know better than to come around the back of the barn like that after dark. It isn't safe."

I thought it best not to remind him that John had been coming around the back of the barn like that to visit us for more than thirty years, and Jack had yet to find it necessary to draw down on him. Some things were best left unsaid.

John stepped onto the porch and took off his baseball cap. "Jack tells me you've got several kinds of desserts left over from when you were, uh, indisposed," he said. "He invited me over to help you get rid of 'em before they spoil."

"Sure thing. What would you like, chocolate pie, chocolate

cake, chocolate pudding, or chocolate cookies?"

I pushed up with my cane, happy that moving was somewhat easier after the brief rest.

"Anything chocolate will do," he said and sat down in the rocker. "Surprise me."

I looked at Jack. "Same for me," he said.

As I stepped into the kitchen, Jack was warning John to be more careful about approaching the back of the house. Men.

I made it back with a tray loaded with several choices tucked under one arm. If they wanted tea or coffee, Jack would have to transport that. I could only carry so much.

John took cake and pudding and Jack grabbed for the chocolate pie, ignoring the fact that out of eight pieces he'd already had five over the last couple of days. I was left with chocolate walnut brownies, my favorite.

We discussed the weather, the recent increase in the population of John's herd, the outrageous price of gasoline, and whether or not Jack was available to help John string some new fencing behind the pole barn in order to keep the new calves from visiting us.

"I'm staying home all day tomorrow," I assured Jack, "so I won't need you. Give John a hand." They set a time to begin work the next morning.

I was getting pretty sleepy by the time John stood to leave. He reached down for his baseball cap and the brown paper bag he'd come in with. Most likely some late summer corn, which would be a very welcome addition to dinner tomorrow night.

"Almost forgot, we had a substitute mail carrier a few days back," John said, "and I got some of your mail by mistake. You get any of mine?"

He reached into the sack and pulled out a magazine, a box of my favorite flavored coffee that I'd been about to sue the company over for non-delivery, and a couple of business sized envelopes. Thankfully, they didn't look like bills from the hospital. We had insurance, but hospitals weren't known for their patience with insurance companies. Well, they weren't going to scare me into paying them and waiting for a refund. We'd already paid the hefty deductible.

Jack leaned around the kitchen door and retrieved John's misdirected mail from the nearby counter. The mail person's errors had now been corrected.

John left and Jack put the ears of corn in the sink for me to clean in the morning. I suggested we head up to bed soon. I didn't often watch the late news any more. Too unsettling and I was having enough trouble sleeping.

"Want anything before bed?" Jack asked as I hobbled to the counter and picked up the mail.

"Are you kidding? I'll be lucky if I get to sleep before daylight with all that chocolate."

"Me, too. Etta makes a mean chocolate pie. If I wasn't already married to you—"

He got another swat on the arm with the latest issue of House And Garden for that remark.

"Don't forget, John's single," I said. "You could just as easily be replaced."

"Don't remind me. I'll be tied up helping him most of the day tomorrow, and there's no one in his lonely old kitchen to bring us lunch. I don't suppose—"

"I'll fix some sandwiches," I said with a sigh. "I'm not quite up to hauling casseroles around just yet. Give me a few more days."

"I'll give you the rest of my life." He hugged me.

I'd give him mine as well, assuming Cousin Will Ann's killer let me.

I might've actually made it to sleep by daylight, if I hadn't decided to open the box of coffee so Jack could get the pot ready for morning. He tossed the empty shipping carton into the trash and reached for the two long envelopes to toss in as well. We were more than ready for Congress to pass a junk mail bill similar to the "Do Not Call" that had given us peace, at long last, during our evening meals. But at least all unwelcome mail could be quickly dumped into the trash.

As the long envelopes bounced into the plastic bag lining the trash can, the return address of the one on top caught my eye. Clete Washington, Private Investigator.

Private investigator? What was a private investigator doing writing to us?

I fished the envelope out of the trash can and the lid swung back and forth as I read the envelope. Actually, it was addressed to me. I was stumped. The name wasn't familiar and the envelope looked suspiciously like a bill.

Jack came back into the kitchen from letting the cat in and locking up the porch. "I thought that was junk mail. Did I throw away the wrong thing again?"

I very nearly said "no" and tucked it into my apron pocket, but the time for holding anything back between us was long past. Whatever time we had left together had to be spent in closeness, and that didn't happen with secrets. I handed him the envelope.

"What is it?" he asked, turning it over.

"I have no idea, but it's from a private investigator and I don't recognize the name. Are you having me followed?" I grinned at him so he'd know I was joking. Jack loved to make jokes but didn't always recognize it when one was tossed his way.

"No," he said, "but it's a mighty good idea. Wonder what this guy charges."

"Open it and see. This looks like a bill."

Jack tore open the envelope, and I quickly found out where I'd been going on the morning of my accident.

CHAPTER THIRTY-ONE

Early the next morning I dressed carefully for my meeting with the private investigator. Like a teacher who wasn't about to be intimidated by some oversized high school boy who'd failed a couple of grades and now towered over everyone else, including the principal.

The long envelope I'd fished out of the trash last night had indeed contained a bill for two hundred dollars, that outrageous amount apparently being the investigator's fee for the client's first half-hour consultation. Which I had no intention of paying. Unless, of course, he was willing to give me the information I'd been after in the first place on the day I'd had the accident.

Jack insisted on going with me. John's fence would have to wait, but I'd had his calves meander into my flower garden before. A wave of my old white apron was generally enough to send them running back home to their mommas.

Neither of us said much of anything on the trip to Paducah, except when Jack flat-footed refused to drive to the investigator's office via the Brookport Bridge. "No use tempting fate," he informed me, as he zipped onto I-24 at the outskirts of Metropolis and gassed the car quickly up to highway speed.

The bowling ball in my stomach appeared to be growing, or reproducing, or whatever bowling balls in stomachs did. I went over the private investigator's rather snippy letter in my head. It was in my purse—not the gingham one, this occasion called for black leather—but I already knew the contents of the letter by heart. Because the investigative firm had a "must cancel no less than twenty-four hours before appointment" policy, I was being billed for a thirty minute consultation, which appointment, according to the letter, I'd not only rudely neglected to keep, but I'd also not bothered to observe the courtesy of phoning to cancel.

Courtesy, shmertesy, I certainly would have called and cancelled my appointment twenty-four hours in advance, had I but known that someone was going to try to kill me. And I planned on giving Clete Washington that information, possibly along with a piece of my mind. Did the good private investigator think I could see into the future?

As if reading my mind, Jack said, "Kitty, don't get your girdle in a wad. You have to be on your best behavior. I'll talk the guy out of the fee, but if you make him mad he might not tell us what it was you were going to see him about."

"Thank you, Jack, but you needn't have worried. I haven't worn a girdle since nineteen sixty-two." He was right, as usual, but I wasn't about to admit that out loud.

We crossed the bridge, took the proper exit, and hummed around the north side of Paducah, on the Loop. It took a couple of drives around the block to locate Clete Washington's office. He was situated in what was known as Paducah's "Lower Town," an area not far from the river, filled with neglected wonderful old houses, many of which dated back to the eighteen hundreds.

During the last several years, Paducahans had started buying the houses and restoring them to their former luster. That was a project dear to my heart, even though I lived across the river in another state. I simply couldn't bear to see any of the older buildings lost to what some considered to be modern progress.

My opinion of Clete Washington went up several notches as soon as Jack pulled up in front of his office. A magnificent old home, it had one of those gigantic round turrets in the front that I'd always envied in old houses. The fussy white gingerbread trim set off well against the yellow shingles that turned warm in the morning sunlight. Begonias lined the sidewalk up to the huge light grey porch that fronted the house up to the turret, and beneath the front windows the late-blooming summer garden fairly made my hands itch to pick and prune and dead-head and simply enjoy.

Jack took my arm and steered me quickly by an inviting bench under a huge maple tree. "We're here on business, remember? No time to sit in the yard and dream."

I let him lead me past, but Private Investigator Clete Washington would indeed be lucky if he didn't come outside early some morning to find me on all fours in the middle of his garden. My own flower garden had suffered a bit of neglect since the accident, and I grieved for that. Maybe now, with the cane instead of the walker, I could get down into the earth and bring my flowers back to life. I'd certainly have to give it a try.

We stepped inside and were greeted by a rather sulky teen-aged girl with long black braids all over her head. I wondered why she wasn't in school until I remembered it was Saturday.

"I'll tell Daddy you're here," she said, turning to the intercom.

I glanced around at the reception area. Inside the bowed-out turret were some comfortable looking, older leather chairs, and the matching couch squatted in the middle of the reception area. Nearby tables held dog-eared copies of National Geographic. Three lush ferns filled the rest of the turret, soaking up the sunlight that filtered through the lace curtains. Nothing fancy here, but well taken care of. I drooled over the carved mantle that surrounded the fireplace and wondered if the firm ever used the gas logs inside.

Washington came out of his office and greeted us. Far from a hulking, failing, high schooler, this man was short, narrow, and well-dressed in a tan jacket and slightly darker pants that matched his skin tone. I envied his smooth skin and obvious lack of wrinkles, though he must be at least as old as Jack and me, if not older, judging from the salt and pepper hair. He ushered us into his office while giving instructions over his shoulder to his receptionist-slash-daughter to hold his calls.

"Momma's coming in to take over for me in a little while. I'm going to the mall with my friends," she said. "I'll tell her you've got clients." The way she said "clients" made me wonder if he had all that many.

I also wondered how many calls an older PI got per day. He didn't look strong enough to chase down deadbeat husbands or fathers. Or repossess cars by snatching them away from angry owners, if that's what he did. I hoped he'd give us a little background on himself.

I was suddenly no longer angry. Chances were, his wife had written that letter and sent the bill. Neither had been hand signed, and he likely needed every fee he could get his hands on. I'd hold my tongue for once in my life and see what he had to offer us.

"I'd pretty much given up on you coming to see me, Mrs. Bloodworth." Washington sat down in a large, slightly cracked, leather chair, leaned on his ancient oak desk, and folded his hands together. His comfortable air made it impossible to be in awe of him.

"Mr. Washington," Jack began, "from what your letter says, apparently Kitty was on her way to see you recently. Just after crossing the Brookport Bridge, she was involved in a serious car accident. She spent a lot of time in the hospital and she's still in therapy."

Jack glanced at me, and I nodded, happy to let him take the lead while I watched Washington for his reactions. I could usually read people pretty well. He was interested, but not impressed, not just yet. For all he knew, this could be a fairy tale. I was sure he'd pretty much heard every excuse known to man. Or woman.

"Kitty hadn't told anyone of her appointment with you, so we didn't even know we needed to cancel it. And frankly, at that time we were pretty much focused on just keeping her alive. It never occurred to me afterwards to try to find out if she was expected anywhere that day."

"I see," Washington said.

I wasn't at all sure he did. Time for me to help out.

"Mr. Washington, the problem is, I was trapped in the car for an entire day and night. By the time they got me to the hospital, I was running a high fever from a collapsed lung." No need to mention the broken leg. He'd looked over my cane as I'd limped to my chair.

His eyes widened as I spoke. Now I really had his attention.

"That explains why we couldn't contact you," he said. "I was doing some surveillance around then, and I remember hearing about a driver being trapped overnight near the bridge. But I never caught the name. I'll tell my wife to void the charge for that first visit. You do understand I'll have to charge you for my time today."

His well-modulated voice would have matched any high school English teacher far better than a private investigator.

I swallowed a giggle at the sudden vision of this sophisticated-looking gentleman lurking in bushes, taking pictures of erring spouses. Had Cousin Will Ann hired him to follow Craig and Sunny? If so, she'd better be glad she was already dead.

"I tried to call your home number and received no answer," Washington said. "In this business, that generally means someone has caller ID and doesn't want me to contact them by phone. We thought probably you had changed your mind about consulting us and had cut off any contact. My wife insisted on sending you a bill. She's very protective of this business and tends to overreact."

Uh huh. And he didn't seem to object to her doing that. But I couldn't blame him. He'd set aside time for me, and I'd kept him waiting. Maybe he'd be willing to barter.

I nodded. "Of course. And I do need some information from you today. That's why we came. I can't remember anything that happened to me for at least a week before the accident. So I have no earthly idea why I made an appointment with you."

Well, I had a rough idea that it had to do with Cousin Will Ann's murder. Jack and I had gone over that possibility this morning with our cereal and coffee. But no need to play all my cards at once. Might as well see if he knew why I'd made the appointment.

"Do you have any idea why I was coming to see you? Had I given you any information over the phone?" My palms were sweating. I hoped I'd not been cagey with him or his receptionist when I'd originally made the appointment.

"Unfortunately, no, I don't. You told my wife that it was personal and you'd have to see me before you could explain." He looked at Jack, maybe sizing him up as to whether or not he was a cheater, and how easy he would be to follow. I decided to level.

"A few days before my appointment with you, my cousin died," I said. "She was murdered. Her name was Will Ann Lloyd. Does that ring a bell?"

He blinked. "I really couldn't say, Mrs. Bloodworth. We keep our clients' identities and information very confidential here. If we didn't, we'd soon be out of business."

I wasn't satisfied. I could tell Jack wasn't either.

"Kitty would never have made an appointment with you about me or anyone else in our family," Jack said. "She can detect what any one of us is doing at any given time without the least bit of help from anyone else. It's impossible to keep anything from her."

Yeah, never mind that Jack had kept the knowledge of his tumor away from me. We had an appointment with the doctor Monday to get the results of the biopsy. It was going to be a very long weekend.

Washington said, "I'm sorry, but I can't help you folks out. I can't tell you anything about my other clients."

"Look, Mr. Washington," I said, jumping back in. "My family tells me that Mrs. Lloyd stormed into a meeting we were attending the night she died and made remarks about our daughter, Sunny Bloodworth. She'd been threatening to have her son followed to see if he was dating our daughter. Mrs. Lloyd is dead now, so she doesn't need confidentiality. The police are investigating her murder. We simply want to know if she had you follow her son, Craig Tanner, or our daughter."

Washington's eyes widened again. I'd struck a nerve somehow. I leaned forward and the chair wobbled.

"I will gladly pay your fee for the first appointment that I missed, as well as for today, if you'll give us some hint as to whether or not Mrs. Lloyd was a client of yours." I looked helplessly at Jack. He squeezed my hand.

"Mr. Washington, we have reason to believe Craig might somehow be involved in his mother's murder," Jack said. "And that would involve our daughter. They're good friends. We only want to know if you followed our daughter and whether or not she was somehow mixed up in Mrs. Lloyd's murder."

Washington leaned back in his chair and put his thumbs in the arm holes of his vest. I could see that his suit wasn't expensive, but it was well-kept and his wife certainly had good taste in ties.

"Who is the detective in charge of Mrs. Lloyd's case?" Washington asked.

"His name is Parker," Jack said.

"Handcuffs Horace?" Washington's eyes twinkled and a broad grin spread across his face. "I haven't seen him in years, in spite of the fact that his office is less than two miles from here. I trained that rookie!" He shook his head and reached for the intercom.

"Raven, you still out there?"

"Yes, Daddy," the bored-beyond-bearing voice replied.

"Call the Paducah Police Department. Tell them Clete Washington needs to speak to Detective Horace Parker and that it's urgent."

She didn't dignify the request with an answer, so we all sat in hopeful silence for a couple of minutes until the phone beeped at Washington's elbow.

"Handcuffs, how are you?" Washington asked. He listened for the reply and deep laughter rolled out from somewhere under his tie tack.

"Listen, I understand you boys are investigating the Lloyd murder. The body that was found at the car show? I've been reading about it in the newspaper." Again he listened for a response.

"I've got some people here in my office. A Mr. and Mrs. Bloodworth. I think you'd better come on over, if you're free. Mrs. Lloyd was evidently a client of mine." He paused. "Right, but she was here under another name. Tanner. If you'll come on over, I'll give you a copy of the file."

Apparently "Handcuffs" agreed, because Washington hung up and offered us coffee. Before I could decline he assured me it was decaf and that he'd personally brewed it and that it was the Starbucks brand.

"I have to drive to the mall every week or so and buy a fresh supply, but it's worth it," he said. I certainly couldn't disagree with that.

Jack politely declined, but I was more than happy to accept. After all, with the fee we were paying this guy I needed some Starbucks. I just hoped he'd thought to get some of their delicious chocolate biscotti. He had. And I prayed that whatever he had to share with Parker didn't somehow involve our daughter.

Jack was standing and staring out of the window, jiggling the change in his pocket, but I was as happy as a pig in slop by the time Parker strode in with wind-blown hair and flushed cheeks. At least I was until he slapped a search warrant for Craig's apartment down on Clete Washington's desk.

CHAPTER THIRTY-TWO

"I hope you have some interesting information for me, Prez," Parker said. "Doesn't really matter, we're pretty sure the boy killed his momma, but anything you can give me might help convict him."

With that Parker dropped into a chair and nodded to us. I was too angry and frightened to nod back. What had made "us" suddenly so certain Craig was guilty? It was all I could do not to spit Starbucks all over Washington's desk.

"For the last time, Handcuffs, I was not named after the first president. I was named after Booker T. You'd do well to remember that. I can still cuff you with one hand tied behind my back."

I was fascinated to see Parker blush. So that was how he'd gotten the nickname? I filed that for future reference.

Clete Washington reached into a metal file holder on the shelf next to his desk, came out with a red file, and opened it.

"My wife likes to use bright colors to differentiate between the active cases and the inactive. I put this up here so she could change it to inactive, but she hasn't been well this week. Raven's been doing her momma's job whenever I can chain her to the desk chair. She much prefers the mall."

Actually, I much preferred the mall to a private investigator's office myself, but now was not the time to express that.

Washington adjusted his glasses and glanced through the first few pages of the report. "Mrs. Tanner, or Mrs. Lloyd, which ap-

parently was her real name, hired me a month or so ago to follow her son around. She wanted me to find out who he was
dating. And if it was serious."

"And?" Parker prodded.

"Well, near as I could tell, the boy wasn't dating anybody.
And I told her that."

"Nobody at all?" I asked.

Washington nodded. "He was seeing a lot of your daughter,
Mrs. Bloodworth, but they didn't seem to be actually dating. I
mean he never took her out to eat or to a movie or anything.
Mostly he went to her place or she went to his. But they always
had books under their arms, or a back pack. I followed them to
the library a few times."

"So, nothing personal was going on between them that you
could see?" Parker looked disappointed. Personally, I wasn't
surprised. Jack just sat and listened.

"Nope. Just two cousins studying together. At least that's
how Mrs. Tanner . . . Mrs. Lloyd explained their family relationship to me. Cousins."

I started to correct him about the cousin thing, but Jack
tapped my foot with his.

Parker thought that over. "I don't suppose you were following them the night Mrs. Lloyd was murdered?" he asked hopefully.

Washington opened the folder again and consulted the page
on top. "Nope, not that night. Sorry. According to the date on
this, Mrs. Lloyd came in and paid me off on the morning of the
day she died, and she told me she wouldn't be needing me any
more. She seemed very relieved at the other news I'd given
her."

I sat up, and so did Jack and Parker. "Relieved?" we asked in
unison. It might have been funny if I hadn't been so nervous.

Jack tugged me back into my seat, and we let Parker finish

the question. "About what?"

"I'd seen the young lady in question, Sunny Bloodworth, with another guy. Now, those two did look serious. Some heavy kissing and hugging whenever he took her home. So I told Mrs. Tanner that. She thanked me, slapped a nice bit of cash down on my desk, and left. I never saw her again, and I certainly didn't associate her with the murder victim. There weren't any pictures of her in the Paducah Sun."

That was because Patricia Ann hadn't allowed any. She said her mother would have been horrified to make the local newspapers "that'a way" and I'd had to agree.

"Whom did you see our Sunny with?" I moved my foot so Jack couldn't tap me again, but from the way he leaned forward, he wanted to know the name as much as I did.

"I'm sorry, ma'am, I couldn't see his face. It was dark on the porch in front of your daughter's apartment. But he's much taller than Craig Tanner, and much slimmer, so I knew it wasn't him. Since Mrs. Tanner . . . that is, Mrs. Lloyd, paid me off, there was no reason for me to investigate the couple any further."

And I had to be satisfied with that. Detective Parker stood. "I'm still going to execute this search warrant and see if we can come up with anything at Craig's place." He turned to me. "Kitty, I'd appreciate it if you wouldn't let Craig know we're coming."

I put on my best injured look, but I was dying to call Craig and warn him.

"Not to worry." Jack stood and shook Parker's hand. "I'll see she doesn't get near a phone, including her cell. You will let us know what happens?"

Parker nodded and left. I was fishing for my checkbook when Washington said, "Mrs. Bloodworth, I didn't want to say anything in front of Ol' Handcuffs, because he tends to grab the ball and run with it, not always looking to see which particular direction his own goal post lies, but I am just a bit concerned about your daughter."

I stopped wading through my purse and gave him my full attention. Jack dropped back into his chair, hanging on every word.

"Concerned about what?" Jack asked.

"The man I saw her with, well, he's no spring chicken. Like I said, I couldn't see much of him, but I've been in this business a mighty long time. It was the way he walked, the way he held himself. This is an older man. And older men with young girls . . . well, let's just say it isn't always a good idea. Most of them are looking to recapture their youth or just be seen with a pretty young thing on their arm. Which means they might not have the young lady's best interests at heart. You know what I mean?"

I nodded and looked at Jack. His eyes narrowed. Not a good sign. He reached out and shook Washington's hand. "Thank you, sir, and you can bet we'll look into this."

"You're most welcome. I'd want to know if my baby girl was dating some guy with a middle-age crisis. I hope it turns out to be nothing."

"It will, count on it," Jack said as we exited the office.

Washington's "baby girl" had her feet propped up on the desk, and was chatting on her cell phone and filing her nails when we entered the reception room. She dropped her feet, tugged down her too-short skirt, and informed the party on the other end of the agency's office hours. Like we didn't know she was talking to someone she shouldn't be.

From the look on Clete Washington's face, she was about to get a lecture she wouldn't soon forget. I dropped the check on her desk and we left them to it. I had a lecture of my own to deliver, just as soon as I could run Sunny to earth.

CHAPTER THIRTY-THREE

Finding Sunny turned out not to be quite as difficult as I'd thought. She was drinking ice tea, relaxing on our sun porch when we got home.

"Don't say anything to her about Parker searching Craig's place," Jack whispered, pulling me back inside the kitchen door. "You know she'll run to tell him, and I'm too worn out to sit on her."

"I won't, but you let me handle asking her about the older man Washington mentioned. Okay?"

Jack reluctantly agreed. I looked out the kitchen window.

"It sounds like Craig is using the tractor again," I said. "At this rate, you won't have to mow until January."

"I'll have to say that boy is nothing if not conscientious when it comes to helping out his family." Jack shook his head. "I sure hope it wasn't him that killed his momma. I don't think I could handle that. And if it turns out to be Craig who ran you off the road, that boy had better run for cover."

That didn't sound good, and I wasn't sure I could handle the truth if Craig was the murderer, either, even though I'd speculated about it. I felt a tear and wiped it away. Time to tackle Sunny. I limped out to the porch and sat down beside her on the futon. The smell of freshly cut grass filled the room.

"Where were you guys?" she said. "I was worried sick. You don't have your cell phone turned on, so I couldn't even leave a message."

"We had an appointment in Paducah," I hedged. "I couldn't leave it on." I put my feet up on the wicker coffee table. My injured leg tended to swell if I was on it too long, and today it was ballooning quickly.

"Want some tea?" Jack shouted from the kitchen, as if we were on John Holmes' porch, several acres away instead of several feet. Maybe he needed to have his hearing checked. He seemed to shout a lot lately.

"Would you mind heating me up a cup of coffee?" I said. "I only had one at breakfast this morning and that tends to leave me cranky."

"Sure," came the reply. "Think I'll have some too."

Great. That would keep him busy for a few minutes.

"Sunny, I'm worried about you."

She turned her attention back to me from watching Craig mowing around the edge of the pond. Honestly, if that tractor got any closer, he'd be mowing the weeds beneath the water. City boys.

"Worried about me? I'm not the one recovering from a serious car accident, Mother."

I noticed she was chewing on a strand of her curly hair, something she always did when she was upset.

"I know you said there is nothing going on between you and Craig," I began. She opened her mouth wide, most likely to argue, but I cut her off. "And I believe you." Her mouth snapped shut. "But you've been seen out with an older man. Your dad and I are worried about you," I repeated.

"Seen by who? Some of Dad's Romeo buddies?"

"Whom," I automatically corrected. "But that doesn't matter. What matters is the identity of the man you're dating, and why you're keeping it such a deep, dark secret. You've never done that before. Ever. You've always been very open with your father and me. The fact that you are keeping this so quiet means there's something wrong. Very wrong."

She turned back to watching Craig, not answering me.

"He's married." I made it a statement, not a question. That was the only reason I could think of for her not to bring this man home to meet us.

She still didn't answer.

"Sunny, your father will be out here any minute with the coffee. I don't want him to know about this if I'm right. But you have to let me know what's going on."

"Oh, Mom, it's such a mess. Please, don't tell Dad. I know you've always taught us that if a woman falls in love with a married man, and he leaves his wife for her, all she's gotten for her trouble is a cheating husband." She scrubbed away the tears on her cheeks.

"Because if he'll do it to her, he'll do it to you," I warned for the hundredth time.

She nodded. "I really didn't mean it to happen, and I swear, it wasn't . . . I mean we haven't . . ." She covered her face and boo-hooed.

"Jack," I shouted at the kitchen door, "see if you can find us some cake in the pantry, or some cookies." That should keep him busy for a few more minutes.

"You haven't been intimate, right?"

She nodded, grabbed for the tissue box on the side table, pulled one out, and blew nosily into it.

"Good," I said. "Then it isn't too late to get out of it."

She wiped her eyes. "I'm trying, honest Mom. But he doesn't want to let go. I mean, he isn't stalking me or anything, just calls to see how I am, or sends me flowers, nearly every day."

"Does Craig know?"

"Huh-uh. I mean, he knows there was someone and that it's over. He's really been supportive. You'd be so proud of him."

187

Indeed I would, if I found out he hadn't killed his own mother.

"I'm glad you have him for a friend, Sunny. But you should've let us know something was wrong."

"I wanted to, but you were recovering from the accident about the time I broke it off, then Dad had his surgery, and the time never seemed right."

"Who is this man? Anyone we know?"

She gave me the look that said I'd crossed the line and stuffed the tissue into her pocket. I wracked my brain, but I'd not seen her giving any particular attention—not even an adoring glance—to anyone we knew. Besides, practically every male we knew was old enough to be more in need of a portable oxygen cart than a lovely young girl. Although, in the Bible, elderly King David did have . . . best not to go there.

Jack stepped onto the porch. He carried a tray with full coffee cups and a mound of cookies. The bloodhound nose that had served Craig Tanner so well throughout his childhood apparently still worked, because he zipped up to the porch on Jack's ancient mower and quickly dismounted. Which meant, at least for the moment, that Jack wouldn't be able to quiz Sunny about her mystery man.

"Got anything to drink?" Craig shouted to Sunny. Then he spotted us. "Oh, hello, Cousin Kitty, Cousin Jack."

"Thanks for mowing the yard, Craig. You've really saved me a lot of work the last few weeks. How'd you get into the pole barn, by the way? I always keep it locked." Jack Bloodworth was nothing if not subtle.

"I gave him my key, Dad. You pretty much burned me out on mowing in high school. When Craig offered to help, I jumped at the chance."

So that was how he'd gotten the key to the pole barn. But had he used it to put his mother's body in there? And if so, how had he opened the trunk? Sunny didn't have any spare keys to Jack's Chevy. No one had them, except me.

Craig took a glass of tea from Sunny and gave her a big smile of thanks. Yep, he had it bad for her. If only she had the sense to see what a good young man he was.

Unless, of course, he was a murderer.

Chapter Thirty-Four

I read all of Dr. Morrison's degrees once again, though by now I nearly knew them by heart. We'd been sitting in his office for several minutes. He'd removed the stitches and pronounced Jack recovered from the surgery, but wanted to talk to us in his private office after Jack got dressed. I didn't figure that was a comforting sign. He could have given us any good news in the exam room. But I didn't share that thought with Jack. He was busy picking lint off his pants and dropping it onto the doctor's lovely Persian rug. I resisted the urge to elbow him. The good doctor surely had a clean-up crew to vacuum up Jack's discarded lint.

Morrison swept in, folder in hand, and dropped into his desk chair. He leaned forward. Yep, it wasn't good news.

"Mr. Bloodworth, the biopsy did show cancer. That's the bad news."

Jack turned pale. I reached for his hand. The bowling ball in my stomach landed at my feet.

"The good news is, it's a very slow growing cancer, the tissue I removed surrounding it was entirely clean, and, most important, the surrounding lymph glands I removed were also cancer free."

"So it hasn't spread?" I asked the obvious. I knew Jack wouldn't think to ask anything.

"No. We're in great shape there."

Why did doctors always say "we" like they had the same

disease? It wasn't all that comforting to the patient.

"What next, chemotherapy?" I asked. Jack just stared at the doctor as if the possibility of cancer had never really occurred to him.

Morrison leaned back in his chair and relaxed, which I took as a good sign. "No, I don't think chemotherapy will be necessary. Radiation is probably the best way to go in this case." He reached for Jack's file. "I had my receptionist set you up with an oncologist here in Paducah. Dr. Lang. That's who I'd go to if I needed cancer treatment."

Jack found his voice. "Will someone have to drive me?"

I knew he was thinking that I wouldn't be able to do it. At least not yet. The therapist still hadn't released me to drive.

"Yes, you'll need someone along."

Jack nodded.

"Maybe Craig can help us," I said. Assuming he wasn't in the slammer for the rest of his life by the time the appointment arrived.

Jack stood and reached for the appointment card. "Thanks, Doc. I appreciate all you've done." He tucked the card in his shirt pocket and turned to the door, leaving the all important questions unasked.

Well, not me. "Will the cancer come back?" I asked.

"Probably not," Morrison said. "But I'd like to see Mr. Bloodworth for a check-up at least every six months from now on. And, of course, you should call me at the first sign of a problem. Other than that, you can go back to life as usual."

He winked at me, making me regret I'd ever asked him the s-e-x question in the first place.

Morrison called out to Jack's back, "And no putting it off this time, Mr. Bloodworth. Call me right away if you have any new symptoms."

Jack turned and smiled. That was all the commitment Morrison was going to get from him. Well, Jack still had me to deal with, and I was on the alert now. He wasn't going to be able to hide so much as an ingrown toenail.

I thanked the doctor and we left. Jack wanted to have lunch while we were still in Paducah, but I opted for Farley's Cafeteria in Metropolis. I was dying for some of their delicious pie, and there was something I wanted to check on. Besides, I hadn't been there since Cousin Will Ann's murder, and I was determined to do the life-as-usual thing, even if it killed me. Well, maybe not literally.

We were able to nab a parking space right in front of Farley's. Jack opened the door for me and helped me up onto the tall curb. Some of the downtown sidewalks in Metropolis had obviously been designed for the horse and buggy generation because their height certainly posed a challenge for anyone getting out of a truck with a cane. Not to mention having to walk around the little decorative chains the city had strung across the edges of some of the curbs to beautify the store fronts. Even though they were only about a foot or two off the ground, I certainly couldn't step across them.

I stood by the truck for a couple of minutes, looking around at the short alleyway beside Farley's where, according to Jack, Cousin Will Ann had parked her Beemer the night of her murder. It was empty now and washed clean by the early morning rain. I turned slowly in a circle, looking around for anything that might jog my memory of the night she died. Nothing happened, so I took Jack's arm and we headed inside for lunch.

The turkey and dressing was as good as anything my momma ever made, and I gobbled it down, getting the hiccups for my poor manners. Jack laughed at me as I gulped a glass of water.

Philby Mason, president of the car club, and his wife Reva came in, and Jack invited them to sit with us as we finished off our pie and coffee.

Reva Mason was still on a walker from a stroke last year, so Philby eased her over to our table and took her order. "Same as they apparently had," she said. "The dressing smells great. And don't forget the homemade bread and butter." He nodded and went to fill their trays from the long line of delicious choices.

We chatted about the recent meetings, all of which Jack and I had missed due to my accident and his surgery. She filled us in on the upcoming Central Division National Fall Meet, which our group was hosting again.

Thankfully, we'd been far enough into the year when I'd had the accident that there weren't any dues coming in for me to record or deposit. But as treasurer I still had a mountain of work to get busy on very soon, so I'd be ready for the fall meet. T-shirts and coffee mugs had to be ordered and paid for, not to mention all the other souvenirs we'd sell to raise money for the club. And all that stuff would have to be sent to my home for sorting and pricing.

"I'll be happy to come out and help you with the sale items," Reva offered.

I could have hugged her. Preparing for the meet was a huge job even for someone in perfect health. For Jack and me, right now it would be nigh unto impossible. I knew we could most likely get several of the others to help out as well.

Philby arrived with Reva's tray, plunked it down in front of her, and made his way back to the food line as she ducked her head for a quick blessing. She opened her silverware package and began sniffing at the food. It very nearly made me hungry again, and I was glad I still had some pie left.

"This place is wonderful," she said. "I'm so glad we meet here from time to time." She blushed like she'd said something wrong.

I hastened to assure her she hadn't. "I love it here, too. This is the first time we've had a chance to come here since my accident. I've missed it."

I glanced up the staircase to the area where we usually met. Reva was looking up there as well.

"Do they have any idea yet who killed Will Ann?" she asked in a low voice.

They did, but I wasn't allowed to tell, not that I wanted to. I just couldn't believe Craig Tanner would hurt his own mother, no matter how caustic she'd been to those around her. So I just shrugged. That wasn't exactly a lie, was it?

"I wasn't at that meeting," Reva said. "The one where Will Ann burst in here and shouted at you. I had a real bad cold. But Philby told me about it. I couldn't believe it when he came home from the contest the next day and said they'd found her body in your trunk."

"Neither could I, but fortunately I still can't remember anything since just before she died," I said.

Reva appeared to ponder that over a swallow of broccoli salad. Philby reappeared, settled his tray on the table, and sat down across from Jack.

"Honey, they probably don't want to talk about this over dinner," Philby said.

"I don't mind, and our dinner's over," I said. Something was tickling around the edge of my brain. Something to do with the staircase. What was it?

"Philby, you were at the meeting that night," I said. "I still don't remember what happened. Jack's given me his version, but I'd appreciate hearing yours."

Reva put her fork down and listened. Philby tucked his napkin into his shirt. Apparently not wanting to run off the other customers, he leaned forward and whispered, "I've never seen Will Ann Lloyd that angry. Except for maybe the day she keyed my old Model T."

He still looked appalled that anyone could even consider doing such a thing. I nodded my agreement.

"She tromped up the stairs, looked around, spotted you two, and pounced," he continued. "I was afraid we'd have to drag her off you."

Without meaning to, I glanced at his portable oxygen tank. I didn't think he'd be up to a whole lot of dragging. Alive and kicking, Cousin Will Ann had made at least three of him.

He took a sip of iced tea. "Anyhow, she spotted you and demanded to know, in a voice that could be heard clear up to the courthouse, where your Sunny was. You said you didn't know." He grinned and placed his tray on the empty table beside us. "I'd have bet that wasn't true, but in your place I'd have done the same thing for one of my kids. Watching Will Ann Lloyd coming straight at you on the warpath was about as much fun as sitting in a French foxhole and watching the approaching German tanks. And just about as safe."

I nodded. "And she called Sunny names, is that right?"

Philby ducked his head. He'd known Sunny since she was in junior high. He'd coached her freshman basketball team his last year before retiring.

"Yes, and I was about to get up and tell Will Ann off when she swung around and marched back down yonder staircase. Then she left. Lucky for her."

My heart warmed at the sight of this old friend ready to defend our baby, even though he couldn't have fought his way through a wet paper towel on a rainy day. I reached across and took his hand in mine, then touched Reva's with my free hand. "I really appreciate you two. You don't know how much."

They'd been to the hospital several times, as had all of the car club, not to mention our friends from church and from the school where I'd taught for many years. The comfort of their prayers and hugs was more than I could ever hope to repay in my lifetime.

Jack stood. "Let's leave these good folks to eat the rest of their dinner in peace, Kitty. I'm pretty well nap-worthy." He tapped his slightly bulging tummy.

I felt like loosening my belt, except I was wearing elastic-waist pants. Wonderful invention. Next to Depends, which, thank heavens, I hadn't had to purchase, yet.

We said our good-byes and headed slowly to the door. I still hadn't managed to pick up any serious speed using my new cane, but it always got lots of admiring glances. I turned to wave at Philby and Reva and glanced up the stairs again. My heart froze.

I couldn't see anything at all of the upstairs portion of the restaurant from right here. Which clearly meant that from up there I couldn't have possibly looked down and seen Cousin Will Ann driving out of the little alleyway beside the restaurant. So why had I told everyone that I had seen her? Had I followed her downstairs? Maybe even outside? What was it that my brain wouldn't let me remember?

CHAPTER THIRTY-FIVE

The next morning after church we swung by Taco Bell for some take-out. Jack adored their tacos. For me it was always the taco salad. We'd arrived at home and I was slipping off my shoes when Detective Parker turned into our driveway.

Thankfully, I'd given up wearing pantyhose after the accident so I didn't have to try to struggle out of them while Parker banged on the front screen door. I should've made that decision ten years ago.

Jack beat me to the door, and by the time I reached the couch, Parker was comfortably seated in Jack's favorite chair, his feet on the ottoman. He was also eyeing Jack's lunch.

"I'd offer you some, but it's hard to share a salad," I said primly.

"I've got extra tacos," Jack offered, and picked up two off the TV tray, leaving the other two for Parker.

I could've kicked Jack's good leg. At the rate we were feeding him, Detective Parker would soon qualify for bed and board.

"We executed the search warrant on Craig Tanner's place," Parker said, losing a bit of chopped tomato off the side of his taco in the process. I passed a napkin to Jack who handed it to Parker.

"Find anything?" Jack asked with his mouth full. Hadn't I taught him anything in forty plus years?

Parker swallowed the last of a taco and wiped grease off his hands with the napkin. "Nothing we could arrest him for or charge him with, but that boy is still my best suspect."

I set my fork down, no longer hungry. Most of the sour cream was gone anyhow. Schadzie hopped onto the couch and sniffed at my tray, but I wasn't about to give her anything this spicy. Didn't she know nursing mothers weren't allowed fiery food? She leaped down, swatting me with her fluffy tail in the process.

"Why are you focusing on Craig?" I asked Parker. "He was with Sunny at the time of his mother's murder. In fact we all have alibis. Why aren't you looking elsewhere?"

Parker swiped his mouth with the napkin, wadded it, and plopped it back on the TV tray. His wife must not run a very tight ship.

"We checked with the pizza delivery company your daughter said she used that night. It was raining hard in Carbondale."

Carbondale was only a little over an hour north of us, but they always got more interesting weather than we did. Rain in dry weather when we had perfectly clear skies, and snow when we only got rain in the winter.

"So?" I prodded.

Parker reached for the other taco. I was definitely going to give Jack a lecture when Parker left. I still wasn't up to kicking speed.

"The delivery guy said the pretty young lady let him step inside, out of the weather. She paid him cash. No one else was there. The apartment is one of those student efficiencies, living room, bedroom, and kitchen all in one area. And even if Craig Tanner had been in the bathroom, the pizza guy would've heard him. It's just to the right of the front door. He said it took her a couple of minutes to dig her wallet out, and then she didn't have enough change, so she dug in a nearby desk and behind the couch cushions to come up with the other forty-six cents."

I'd been in Janet's apartment and there wasn't even enough room to chase a cockroach, and she probably had a couple of roaches, judging by her neatness quotient. I slumped back on the couch.

"What time was the delivery made?" I asked.

"Knew you'd want to know that." Parker reached for his little notebook, and I wondered if he'd been to church before coming out, since he was wearing a rather loud tie.

"According to their phone records," Parker continued, "she called at eight fifteen P.M. and it took about thirty minutes to cook the pizza and get it there. No way she could have been in Metropolis at the time Mrs. Lloyd was murdered, unless she has a rocket ship tucked away somewhere."

I gave him a smarmy smile for his joke, but inside I was relieved. Not that I thought Sunny was capable of killing anyone, but Cousin Will Ann had a way of making people do insane things when she targeted them, and Sunny had been her last target. And me, of course.

"What now?" Jack asked. "Will you arrest Craig?"

"Not arrest, not just yet, but I have asked him to meet me at my office this afternoon."

Then why are you here, eating Jack's lunch? Surely you didn't drive way out into the country on the slim hope of us being home and feeding you?

Parker must've read my thoughts. He turned to me and said, "I just needed to clarify a few things with you folks. I went to Farley's for dinner last night. Took the wife. She loves their roast beef. Anyhow, I went to the upstairs part of the dining room, and guess what?"

I didn't bother guessing, I knew what was coming next. I just wished I'd thought to tell Jack about it.

"You can't actually see through the front door or the side windows from where your table was positioned," Parker announced a bit more triumphantly than I thought necessary. "You would've had to come at least part way down the stairs in order to see Mrs. Lloyd leaving the restaurant or driving out of the alleyway. Just how far did you come down those stairs, Kitty?" He glared at me expectantly.

I shrugged. "Horace, I have no idea. I still don't remember a thing from just before my cousin's murder. If I did, I'd tell you."

And you should've gotten out the rubber hose when you had the chance. Not my fault if it's too late now.

"I checked with the waitresses and the bus boy. No one remembers seeing you follow her out, but I'd still like to know where you were when you saw her driving away."

Join the club, fella.

"Sorry, Horace, I can't help you there. I'd like nothing better than to see this case solved." Assuming the arrest of the murderer didn't involve someone I loved.

Thankfully, Parker was backing out of the driveway when I answered Sunny's hysterical phone call for help.

CHAPTER THIRTY-SIX

"Mother, can you and Dad get over to Hank's house immediately?" Sunny said.

"What's wrong? Did something happen to Hank? Or Craig?"

Dead silence from the other end of the phone. I figured Patricia Ann was probably safe at her place over in Paducah. Craig was still staying with his step-father. So what was going on over there?

I signaled Jack to put his shoes back on and struggled into mine. With a bum leg, even open-backed shoes didn't slip on quite as fast as they came off.

"Sunny? Answer me, what's wrong?"

"Oh, Mom, it's just awful. I'm so ashamed to tell you, but I have no choice. The married man I told you I'd been seeing was Hank."

Say what? She'd been seeing Cousin Hank? I started to say something, but she didn't give me a chance.

"Craig found out about it today and called me. I'll give you the details later, but Hank came in while Craig was shouting at me, and they got into a fist fight."

"Fist fight?" I said.

"Fist fight?" Jack echoed, throwing down the shoe horn. "Tell Sunny to keep up her left, like I taught her. We'll be there in a few minutes." He grabbed his keys.

"Mom, I couldn't call the police. You have to get over there right now and stop them before one of them gets hurt. I'm on my way, but I had to stop for gas in Vienna. My car's empty. I won't be able to get to Hank's for at least another twenty minutes. They could kill each other by then."

"Young lady, you should have told me all of this when I first asked you." I shrugged into my light-weight jacket again. It might be late summer, but I go nowhere without a wrap.

"I know, Mom, and I promise I will tell you everything. Just hurry. I don't want Craig to get hurt . . . or Hank." The fact that she'd mentioned Craig first didn't slip by me.

"We're on our way out the door. I'll call you on my cell phone."

I plugged the cell phone into the lighter socket and speed dialed her number as Jack backed his old truck out of the garage. He demanded to know why we were going to Hank's if Sunny was the one in trouble. He turned and headed down our long driveway.

"She isn't—" I shut the cell phone to interrupt the call and placed a hand on Jack's arm. "Honey, I should have told you this, but she begged me not to. Sunny admitted to me the other day that she'd been seeing a married man."

The truck swerved, nearly hitting the hundred-year-old oak at the edge of our driveway. Jack straightened the wheel, and I continued with my story. "Remember when Sunny was sitting on the porch while Craig was mowing? Right after we left Clete Washington's office? You were getting us coffee. I told her she'd been seen with someone. I asked her who it was, and she admitted she'd fallen in love with an older man. I asked if he was married, since most older men are, and she said 'yes.' She assured me she'd broken it off, and—"

"Who is it? I'll kill him. Does Craig know? I'm going back for my pistol." Jack turned the wheel, but I grabbed his arm again and held it steady.

"Listen, Sunny needs you to be calm right now. And so do I.

No guns and no fist fights. Or I'll let you walk home and handle this all by myself."

Jack gave me his best not-a-chance look. "I know the way to Hank Lloyd's house as well as you do," he said. "You can't send me home because you can't drive yet."

He had a point, but I noticed he slowed down and made the next curve on three wheels instead of two. The road dust was so thick it almost choked me, and the springs on Jack's old truck weren't what they used to be. I continued my story as we bounced and jounced down our gravel country road.

"Jack, she was seeing Cousin Hank. She told me just now. We should've guessed when Washington said he saw her with someone who looked older."

"I'll kill him."

"You'll have to get in line. Craig's already working on it."

CHAPTER THIRTY-SEVEN

Jack bounced the truck over the curb and slid into Hank Lloyd's driveway. We both wanted to run to the front door, but that wasn't currently possible for either of us, so we maneuvered up the concrete steps as fast as we could. The door was standing open and we stepped inside.

Hank was sitting on the floor between the living and dining rooms, holding his right eye. Its upper and lower lid were already nearly as large as half a baseball and swelling quickly. Craig stood over him shouting words I'd washed his mouth out for when he was eleven. He didn't seem to know we were there.

Jack took in the situation and stepped between the two men. "Settle down, boy. This won't solve anything."

"I know, Cousin Jack." Craig paused for a gulp of air. "But he hurt Sunny, and he hurt my mother, and I'm going to make sure he never does it again."

Craig leaned toward Hank, but Jack pushed him away. Jack Bloodworth might be vertically challenged but he still had football player shoulders and knew exactly where to place them for the best effect.

I leaned over, straightened up the small pie table that usually nestled between the French doors and the television set, and placed the pot of ivy back on it. Hank would just have to vacuum up the spilled dirt. He'd gotten himself into this mess . . . literally.

"Craig, sit down and cool off," Jack said. He reached for

Hank's hand and helped him off the floor. "Let's talk this thing over quietly, before the neighbors call the local police. Detective Parker is just dying to arrest you, Craig, and if he hears from a Metropolis officer that you've been fighting, he'll extradite you to Paducah quicker'n you can say 'Miranda.' "

Craig nodded and wiped the blood away from his mouth where Hank had apparently scored a punch or two of his own. Land sakes, why did men always think the only way to settle things was with their fists?

As Craig sat on the arm of the large chair by the fireplace, Hank took a seat on one end of the couch. Jack casually positioned himself between them, and I took a seat near the door.

"Sunny and I were seeing each other," Hank admitted. "We realized it was wrong, Craig, and broke it off well before your mother died. Will Ann never knew, and no one was hurt, except possibly ourselves."

"That's a lie!" Craig jumped up, only to be pushed back down by Jack. "It is a lie, Cousin Jack. Mother called Sunny names the night she died. She must have known something."

She'd apparently called me names too, just a few days before her death, but I didn't figure now was such a great time to bring that up.

"I agree Cousin Will Ann most likely figured out you and Sunny were seeing each other, Hank," I said. "And that's why she caused the scene at Farley's. Are you sure you and Sunny broke if off before she died?" From what Sunny had said, I wasn't exactly sure when the breakup came.

Hank took out a handkerchief and placed it over his enormous eye. "Positive. I told Sunny I didn't want to hurt my dear wife and she agreed. That was at least a week before Will Ann died. We stopped seeing each other right then."

Craig pulled a wadded piece of paper out of his back pocket.

"Then why are you still sending Sunny flowers?"

The hair on the back of my neck stood up. Sunny had said that the man kept sending her flowers, even after she broke it off. So Hank was lying to us.

Craig passed the paper to Jack, who studied it and passed it to me. It was a bill from Rainbow Flowers out on Highway 45, and the total amount for the past month took my breath away. Hank had sent Sunny roses every single day since the day after Cousin Will Ann died. How thoughtful.

I handed it over to Hank. No matter if he destroyed it, the florist would have a record. I tilted my head and gave him my best would-you-care-to-explain-your-way-out-of-this-one look. It had always worked on my students and my own children. Not to mention Jack.

Hank looked at it as if he'd never seen the bill. Fat chance.

"Where did you find this?" Hank said to Craig. "When I kindly invited you to stay here while you grieved for your mother, I didn't think you'd snoop into my personal mail." Hank glared at his stepson.

"I found it on the floor under mother's desk when I was vacuuming this morning. I thought I'd help you out with the housework while you were at church. Good thing I did."

Hank was stalling and Jack was letting him. Give him enough rope . . .

No one said anything for several minutes, and sure enough Hank got antsy.

"After Will Ann died I realized just how empty my life was without Sunny, and how much I really loved her. There was no longer any reason for us to be apart. I want to marry Sunny, after a decent period of mourning passes, of course."

Hank had realized all that in less than twenty-four hours after his wife was murdered? How dumb did he think we were?

"I know this sounds terrible," Hank said, "but you all know I had nothing to do with Will Ann's murder. I have witnesses to prove where I was that night. And our marriage was over a long time ago. Why shouldn't Sunny and I be happy?"

"Because I'm no longer in love with you, and I don't think I ever really was." Sunny stepped through the front door.

I knew I should've shut that door when I came in. What if the neighbors overheard?

"I think I felt sorry for the way Cousin Will Ann treated you," Sunny said. "You played on my sympathy, and to my shame I let you. But that's all over, and I don't want any kind of relationship with you now or ever."

The sun shining through the open door set her auburn hair on fire, and her brown eyes were bright with angry tears. I'd never been prouder of my daughter. I looked at Craig as he stood to go to her. Hank shrugged when Craig hugged her. So much for his deep, abiding love for our daughter.

I'd bet Clete Washington was right. Hank had wanted a pretty young thing on his arm to show off, or to make him feel younger. Unless I missed my guess—and I didn't often—Hank Lloyd would be re-married before Christmas to some poor trusting soul. Unless he was doomed to repeat his mistakes rather than learn from them, and he married another Will Ann Lloyd. But could there ever be another like her?

The fracas appeared to be over, at least for the moment. Craig was murmuring about gathering his things and going back to Carbondale with Sunny. I heard something about pizza. Did those two never eat anything else? She followed him up the stairs to help him pack. Jack and I sat in an uncomfortable silence with Hank until they came back down with a full duffle bag under each of Craig's arms. Sunny carried his books and laptop.

"Patricia Ann already gave me most of Mother's things that I was supposed to have," Craig said to Hank. "You can contact me through my mother's lawyer if you have anything else to say." With head high, Craig marched out to his car, loaded it, and drove off, with Sunny following closely behind in her car.

"Could we keep this mess between us?" Hank asked.

I opened my mouth to give him a piece of my mind, but Jack cut me off. "Of course, Hank. We're no more eager for news of your relationship with Sunny to get out around town than you are."

Hank nodded. "Thank you both for coming. And I want you to know it wasn't all like Sunny said. She encouraged me to confide in her when Will Ann's behavior toward me became unbearable. Otherwise this never would have happened. And I never allowed it to sink into a physical relationship. I stayed strictly hands-off with Sunny."

Hank checked the handkerchief for blood, but there was none. I was happy to see that his eye was still swelling. He was going to have to come up with a whopper of a "walked into a door" story.

"I was going to ask Will Ann for a divorce," he continued, "but then I realized I wanted to be here with her, in order to work things out. Besides, Sunny wasn't quite ready for a mature relationship. So we called it off. You don't have to worry. I won't call her or send any more flowers."

Jack pulled himself up to his full height, which was still well below Hank's and mine. "I think that's the best idea I've heard all day." He started for the door, but Hank reached out to shake his hand.

"Thanks for coming. I owe you one."

"Yes, you certainly do owe me one, Cousin Hank," Jack said. And with that, Jack Bloodworth threw one of the finest uppercuts I'd ever seen, straight into Hank Lloyd's very aristocratic nose. There was an awful lot of blood and it kind of looked like Hank's nose was going to be permanently off center.

CHAPTER THIRTY-EIGHT

"Let's have breakfast at Smallman's," I suggested, early the next morning.

"And why should we drive all the way from here to there, five whole miles, just for breakfast, when we have biscuits and sausage in the fridge, and I'm prepared to step up like a man and fix them for you?" Jack leaned against the kitchen counter.

I was tempted. Boy, was I tempted. Jack Bloodworth could make sausage gravy that would've put my Grandmother Halliburton's to shame.

"Because we haven't been out to breakfast in a long time," I hedged.

"No, because you have something in mind, and I go nowhere until you spit it all out." He crossed his arms over his chest. This might take some persuading.

"Okay, I thought we'd just casually drop by the Metro Chamber before breakfast and check out Cousin Hank's alibi for ourselves."

Jack frowned so I hurried on. "Look, we now know he had a real motive. He wanted Sunny. And, apparently Cousin Will Ann knew about them, judging from her behavior that night. We simply have to know if it was possible for him to have gotten to Cousin Will Ann while he was at that meeting, and she was yelling at us in Farley's."

"But you saw her drive away that night. You said so, right after Parker started questioning us. I remember that much for you," Jack argued.

"But you heard what Parker said yesterday. I couldn't have possibly seen anything if I'd stayed all the way upstairs. I must have come down at least part of the way. Maybe I followed her outside." I gritted my teeth. "Maybe I had a fight with her or something."

"In the first place, Dick Tracy, you were only gone a few seconds after she left. I watched for you while I tried to calm the rest of the members down. You went part way down the stairs, and then you came back up."

That, at least, was comforting.

"And if you did see her drive away," Jack added, "then Hank couldn't have gotten to her. And she died several minutes later. He was at the meeting until ten thirty. Everyone said so. Couldn't have been him. Maybe some stranger caught her off guard."

"Not likely. She'd have sent them off with a serious injury of some sort."

But had I actually seen her drive away that night? If I could only remember.

"Look, we'll just pop into the chamber," I said, "ask a couple of questions, and be on our way to breakfast. Or stop by on the way home, but I really think—"

Jack held up his hand. "I give. Smallman's it is. Because you are not going to be satisfied until we check this out."

He reached for his jacket. Retirement age had made him nearly as cold-bodied as me. Used to be we fought over the thermostat, me turning the heat up, him turning it back down, during the winter months. Now we fought primarily over the quilt Jack's mother helped me make to keep us warm in bed.

Jack spotted an empty parking space right in front of the chamber—practically unheard of—and swung in. Our town is small, about seven thousand residents, but we get tourists from all over wanting to check the Superman statue out. It was rare, indeed, to find a downtown parking spot during daylight hours. The fact that Farley's was only two doors away from the chamber just made it worse. I'd have suggested breakfast there, but Farley's didn't open until lunch, and Smallman's biscuits were hard to beat.

Jack helped me up the curb, and we sallied in. I caught a glimpse of chamber manager Nancy Oliver's lovely white hair and wondered again if I should stop dying mine. The awful growing-out process always kept me coloring. Nancy's volunteer assistant, Catherine, was busy on the phone giving directions to a tour bus driver.

I'm not one to beat around the bush, or anything else, so I dove right into the reason for our visit. "Nancy, I know you talked to the Paducah police, but we just wanted to double-check that there was no way Hank Lloyd could have left the meeting the night my cousin Will Ann was killed."

"I don't see how." She pointed over her shoulder. "We were all in the big back room, gathered around the conference table, and he never left."

Catherine put her hand over the receiver and said, "I don't see how he managed to go three hours without his pipe. He generally has to interrupt meetings by stepping outside. He isn't allowed to smoke it in here."

"Well, thanks, I guess that does clear him."

"Did you have reason to think he might be involved?" Nancy asked. "I always thought he was crazy about Will Ann. Can't figure out why." She blushed.

"We never could figure it out either, so don't let that worry you," I said.

I looked around for Jack. He was browsing the shelves on the wall, obviously hunting for something Tori or Billy didn't already own that had a picture of Superman printed on it. He was such

211

a sucker for those kids. Surely they had every single thing the chamber had to offer in the way of toys or souvenirs by now.

He picked up two small balls that were a clear sort of jell with a picture of Superman in the center, and bounced one off the floor. It nearly hit the twelve foot ceiling. Maggie was going to just love this. Well, it was her father's doing, not mine.

Catherine hung up the phone and came to the cash register to take Jack's money. "I almost wish Hank had been able to smoke that night. He was very restless, pacing the floor a whole lot while we made some very simple preliminary decisions."

I found that interesting. Hank wasn't given to pacing, in general.

Jack took the sack from Catherine and headed to the door. "C'mon, woman, let's eat."

He knows I hate it when he calls me "woman." Like he's a caveman. I put my hands on my hips, but he just grinned. Lucky for him, that grin still made my heart do flips.

"See you ladies later," he called from the front door. I figured I might as well hobble along too.

As I pushed open the door, I thought of another question. "How many of you were here for the meeting that night? Were all of the board members present?"

Nancy said, "No, there were just five of us." She ticked them off on her fingers. "Catherine, myself, Hank, and Jeff and Jeanie Cross. Everybody else had other fish to fry. And it was just a preliminary meeting for next year's festival."

I walked back to the counter. "You said Hank never left the meeting room. What about the rest of you? Surely you didn't stay back there the entire time?"

"No, we were up and down like kids on pogo sticks," Nancy said. "Getting something to snack on, getting coffee, using the bathroom."

"And smoking," Catherine added. "Like I said, members

aren't allowed to do that in here." She pulled up her long blonde hair and fanned the back of her neck. It was pretty hot in here. Old downtown buildings were difficult to heat and cool.

"And neither of you ever saw Hank go outside?" I asked. They both shook their heads. "Is it possible that all of you were moving around at the same time and didn't see him step outside?"

They thought that over. "Yes, it might have been possible," Catherine said. "You know, at one point when I came out of the bathroom, Hank was standing by the back door. I asked if he was going out for a smoke, but he said he'd given up his pipe. Said he was just waiting in line for the bathroom."

"What time was that?" My stomach bounced the bowling ball around a few times.

"Somewhere between eight thirty and nine, I think. We took a break about then, but I didn't look at the clock," Catherine said.

"So he could have gone outside for a few minutes and no one would have seen him go?"

"It's possible, but I couldn't swear to it. I never saw him leave." She thought a minute. "But he and I were the only ones in the meeting room right then. Nancy had come in here to make a couple of phone calls, and Jeff and Jeanie were counting T-shirts in a box that was in here so we'd know whether or not to order more. Hank insisted on the count."

"And the back door is left unlocked during meetings?" I asked.

"Yes. In case someone needs to get something from their car. Members park in the alleyway for meetings."

"And they smoke out there," Nancy said, "But Hank said he'd stopped smoking. I didn't see him take his pipe out at all that night."

But I'd seen him take it out right after Cousin Will Ann's

murder, at home when Parker had questioned him. And I'd seen him do it since. So he certainly hadn't stopped smoking it for good.

"Thanks, ladies, you've been a big help. Could we keep this little visit between us?"

"You're welcome, and we won't say a word to anyone," Nancy called to my back as I hustled to the door as quickly as my cane would allow.

Breakfast at Smallman's would have to wait. Jack and I had a visit to make.

CHAPTER THIRTY-NINE

Naturally, Jack put his foot down and refused to visit Hank and question him about Cousin Will Ann.

"He won't be home," Jack said.

"Yes, he will. He's been working a lot from home since Cousin Will Ann died. Plus, he took some time off to settle her affairs."

"He won't talk to us. Not after I rearranged his nose for him."

"Yes, he will. I'll threaten to call Detective Parker over if he doesn't."

"He couldn't have gotten to Will Ann. He never even went outside that night, according to Nancy and Catherine. And even if he did, how did he know Will Ann would be there?"

"Yes, he could have gone outside," I argued. "If you hadn't left so quickly just now, you'd have heard Catherine say the back door was unlocked and he was standing near it when she came out of the bathroom. Nancy and the others had gone up front for several minutes to do something. And Cousin Will Ann could've paged him. Pagers can be silenced. No one would have known."

Jack clamped his jaws shut, apparently out of arguments for the moment.

"Cousin Will Ann was angry when she came to Farley's because she couldn't get in touch with Sunny," I continued in an effort to sway him to my way of detecting. "What would be her next, most logical move?"

Jack didn't answer my question, so it was up to me to do it.

"She'd go looking for Cousin Hank, and she was bound to have known he was at that meeting. The board members meet the same time every month. Even I know that."

"Then why didn't anyone see her when she went into the chamber?" Jack asked, as he turned onto Highway 45, headed toward Smallman's and away from Hank's house.

I decided to let him drive. We could always go by Hank's on our way home. "Because she wouldn't have gone in. She wouldn't have wanted them to see her confront Hank about another woman. Confronting us about Sunny in public was one thing. You notice she never mentioned Hank's name that night. Confronting him in public about Sunny would be totally different. She'd want to do that in private. Like in the alleyway between Farley's and the Metro Chamber."

"But you saw her drive away. So she was still alive, and Hank didn't leave the meeting long enough to follow her anywhere. So how did he do it? He was at the chamber for a good hour and a half after she left Farley's."

"I haven't quite figured that out, yet. I just want to talk to him and see what we can find out."

"Well, you aren't going to find out anything before I've had my breakfast. My medication says 'Take with a meal,' and that's exactly what I aim to do."

He had me there, so I rode in silence the rest of the way to Smallman's, trying to figure out just exactly how Hank did kill Cousin Will Ann. Because I was convinced by now that he had.

Two eggs over easy, some crisp bacon, a side of hash browns, and a couple of biscuits and gravy later, I thought I had the answer. Amazing what a little sustenance will do for the brain.

"She wasn't driving the Beemer, he was," I said, and Jack nearly spit out a large swallow of coffee. Black, with sweetener.

"That isn't possible. Hank was at the meeting. How many times do I have to remind you of that?"

"She could've paged him and sent him a text message to meet her outside the chamber, in the alleyway."

Jack's brow crinkled over the text message part. I could see I was going to have to bring him up to speed about paging at some point.

"And he could've somehow gotten her into the trunk—he is one of the few people larger than she was, not to mention stronger—and then driven out of the alleyway and around the corner. Then he could've sneaked back into the chamber. It wouldn't have taken more than a couple of minutes."

Jack chewed on that along with the rest of his biscuit.

"And even if she'd been alive in that trunk," I continued, "if he pulled around the corner and parked, not a soul would've heard her screaming. You know how deserted downtown is at night. All of the people in Farley's parked on the street in front. The board members all parked behind the chamber. If he parked on a side street, no one would have been anywhere near her car."

Jack nodded slowly, still not completely buying it. The important thing was, would Detective Parker buy it? He was the only one with the authority to pounce on Hank. Although I still intended to give it my best shot.

Unfortunately, I was doomed to disappointment. Hank's car wasn't in the driveway when I finally persuaded Jack to drive by there. I used my cell phone to call Parker. He was about as easy to convince as Jack.

"I appreciate your efforts, Kitty. It is interesting that Mr. Lloyd could've gotten out of the chamber that night and not been seen, but the time frame is mighty narrow."

Narrow, schmarrow. Hank Lloyd was quick and strong. And several years younger than Cousin Will Ann. He could have easily overpowered her and tossed her into the trunk and nobody the wiser. Driving and parking around the corner—so no one would see her car—wouldn't have taken much more than a couple of minutes. With the other board members busy, and Catherine in the bathroom, he could easily have made the trip and run back to the alleyway and through the back door. And I told all that to Parker, along with something else that was very difficult.

"He'd been seeing our daughter, Sunny. He was the man your friend Mr. Washington saw her with. But you know she wasn't involved. The pizza delivery guy saw her at home."

"I have to agree, your daughter probably wasn't involved, but I will have to talk to her again. First, I'll give Mr. Lloyd a call and have him come in. And neither you nor your husband are to contact him under any circumstances, understand? This certainly does bear looking into, but we'll handle it from here. Thank you for your—"

And with that, Parker hung up on me. Or the cell phone dropped the call. It was difficult with these new-fangled things to know whether people were being rude or the phone company was. I dropped the phone into my purse and turned to Jack.

"You're in luck. Parker ordered us not to contact Hank. He's taking care of it."

I took the resulting snort as an "I told you so" and turned to watch the clouds over a nearby corn field. I concentrated on them the rest of the way home, so as not to have to wonder if a man I'd known for ages had murdered my cousin and tried to romance my daughter into having sex with him.

I wished I had a digital camera so I could capture some of that magnificent sky. Maybe I could even create one of those lovely coffee table books with pictures of Southern Illinois clouds. If I could catch some over the head of our Superman statue, I'd have a best seller, judging from the number of tourists who annually climbed over and around it, snapping pictures. I wondered how long it would take me to talk Jack Bloodworth into that one.

CHAPTER FORTY

When we arrived home, Jack gave me a peck on the cheek and escaped to his garage. Most likely he'd putter the afternoon away there. I put my purse in the closet and headed to the kitchen. Given our huge breakfast, Jack wouldn't expect me to fix lunch, but I did need to set something out for supper.

While I mulled the various possibilities in the refrigerator, Schadzie weaved in and out of my ankles. I gave in and pulled out the milk carton. Nursing mother or no, if she kept eating at this rate, she soon wouldn't be able to fit through the back door to tend to her babies. So far we'd located two of them stashed inside our well house, one black and long-haired, like mom, and one silver bob-tailed, just like the stray that had taken up residence in John Holmes's barn. I pulled out a couple of frozen chicken breasts and placed them in the sink.

Just as soon as these kittens were weaned, they were going to the humane society for adoption by some loving family, and Schadzie was going to the vet for the permanent birth control fix she should've had long ago. I decided to check on the kittens right now and headed to the sun porch.

To say I was shocked to see Hank Lloyd sitting there in my good rocking chair would be putting it mildly. His Volvo hadn't been in the driveway. How had he gotten here? Had he parked behind the pole barn like Craig always did whenever he helped with the mowing?

"Good morning, Kitty. Have a good breakfast at Smallman's?"

The hair on the back of my neck tingled to attention. I nodded, wondering how I could signal Jack out in the garage. If he started running any of his power tools, he wouldn't hear the angel Gabriel blowing his horn to signal the end of time, much less me signaling that we were apparently about to run out of time. I knew from the look on Hank's face that this was no friendly visit. And the fact that he knew we'd been to Smallman's probably meant he knew we'd been to the chamber. But I had to play along. At least until I could get Jack's attention.

"Hello, Hank. What are you doing here? I figured you'd be too upset with us to come by for a visit anytime soon."

Okay, so it was lame, but I couldn't think of anything better to say. I focused on his nose. He'd evidently been to the emergency room because his nose was covered in a rather awkward white bandage that very nearly made him cross-eyed, and both eyes were as black as a young raccoon's.

"I admit, Kitty, I was upset with Jack yesterday, but I think we're beyond that now, don't you?"

"Of course."

Hank was situated between me and both the kitchen door and the back screen that led outside. No way I could run. Even if I could still run, I was going to have to talk my way out of this situation. Assuming I could. I was a pretty good talker, but I'd never tried talking myself away from a murderer before. Brand new territory.

"Why don't you have a seat, Cousin Kitty, and let's chat?"

"I'd love to, but I'm dying of thirst. I'll just get us a glass of iced tea. Want lemon?"

He reached in his pocket and pulled out the little pistol Cousin Will Ann's mother had given her when she went away to college.

221

"No thanks," Hank said. "It's so pleasant out here, let's just sit." He pointed to the futon.

I eased down on the futon and sat on the edge. My mind was racing. How was I going to get out of this? And what if I couldn't? He was obviously going to kill Jack and me. The girls would lose both of their parents at once. Okay, that's how I'd said I'd originally planned to go—the two of us together—but I hadn't really thought about what it would do to our girls. And our grandchildren? Were they even old enough to remember us?

"Kitty, I had hoped you'd stay out of this, for Sunny's sake, if nothing else. I had to go downtown to the chamber this morning to drop off some papers, and I saw you and Jack walking inside. I went to Hardee's for coffee and waited until you two had time to leave. I'm sure you understand why I wouldn't want to meet you in public." He pointed to his nose, and I nodded.

Had the ladies at the chamber ratted on me? Had they told Hank that I'd been quizzing them about him?

"When I went into the chamber," Hank continued, "Nancy and Catherine seemed awfully quiet. They didn't have a lot to say to me, except Catherine asked how I was doing with my efforts to give up the pipe."

I sat still and let him keep talking. I heard Jack's air compressor kick on. Great, now he wouldn't hear anything if the garage fell in around him.

"I told her I'd fallen off the wagon, so to speak, since my dear wife had died. Then I asked if they'd seen you lately. They said they hadn't. I knew that wasn't so, and I figured you must've found out something." He raised his eyebrows.

Oh, dear. I hadn't thought of that possibility.

"Maybe they just forgot we were in there. It's a busy place." I was backpedaling furiously. "We just went in to pick up a couple of toys for the kids."

"And to pick up some tidbits about me. Don't try to fool me, Kitty. Detective Parker left a message on my cell phone for me to come to his office. I'm not sure I plan to keep that appointment."

"What are you planning to do?" And did I really want to know?

"You and Jack are going to have an accident. Something involving that old, rusty tractor Jack mows with, I think. Then, I'll either face Parker with my innocent act, or I may just take off to a foreign country. One without an extradition treaty, of course."

Of course. He seemed to have this all well thought out.

"Let's go find Jack, shall we?" he said. "I don't have all day."

I had to keep him talking. "Why did you kill Will Ann?"

"I didn't plan to, at least not at that time and in that way."

My eyebrows asked "Well, really?" and he answered the unspoken question.

"My darling wife kept control of all of the money she got from the railroad company when her first husband was killed on their tracks. But she did make me her power of attorney right after our honeymoon. You remember, when she had to have emergency surgery?"

I nodded, afraid to speak, and wiped my sweaty hands on my jeans.

"Afterwards, she insisted I tear that paper up, so I got a blank form, filled it out so it would look real, and satisfied her wishes like I always did. She never went to her stock broker's office, just read the statements when they came in. When the stock market dipped a few years back, I was able to skim a little out of her various accounts and make it look like a loss. She didn't catch on. At least not at first."

Skim a little? I'd have bet he'd skimmed a lot.

Hank stood, and my stomach's bowling ball dropped to my

feet again. I'd be mighty glad when this was over and I was rid of it. Unless, of course, I was dead.

Chapter Forty-One

Hank gestured toward the kitchen door with the gun. I didn't move.

"I must've gotten careless," he said, "because Will Ann eventually found out about the skimming. I pleaded with her, and she forgave me. But she had a hold over me. Jail. The way I used that power of attorney wasn't strictly legal, and judges tend to be cranky about things like that."

"Then she found out about Sunny, right?" I reached for my cane.

"No, I think we'd best leave your cane here. Wouldn't want you whacking me over the head with it. But to answer your question, yes, she found out about Sunny. Stupidity on my part. But she is such a pretty girl."

I wanted to chew him up and spit him out, but for the time being I had to be patient.

He gestured toward the kitchen door again, and I struggled to stand. Maybe I could hit him with a frying pan or something in there. It was worth a try. I moved slowly towards the kitchen with Hank close behind me.

"Will Ann was in a particularly rotten frame of mind around last Christmas," he said. "I suspect you remember?"

Oh, yes, I remembered. She'd ruined Christmas Eve for the entire family with her cuts and digs—I swear, the woman's tongue had a serrated edge—and I'd promised myself that would be our last Christmas meal with her. Odd how things had turned out.

"Your charming daughter felt sorry for me and she called me at work to say so. We met for lunch, and soon we were seeing each other fairly often. Sunny can say she only felt sorry for me, but there was a lot more to it than that."

"And it never occurred to you that your wife would hire a private investigator? Wasn't that a bit optimistic on your part?"

"Yes, I suppose it was. If I'd had any hint that she didn't trust me, I'd have been much more careful."

Of course he would have. "How did Cousin Will Ann find out about you and Sunny? The private investigator told us he didn't know who Sunny was seeing."

"Ah, so you did manage to meet with the private eye? And you didn't mention it to me? I'm truly crushed, Cousin Kitty. Will Ann came to the car lot earlier on the day she died. She rarely did that. I was on the phone trying to talk Sunny into changing her mind about breaking it off with me. Will Ann must've overheard me and become very upset. One of my salesmen saw her leaving in a hurry. I suppose she went looking for Sunny to tell her about my past. When she couldn't find Sunny, she decided she was going to send me to jail in order to keep me away from her. In spite of the fact that she was so angry with Sunny, she still wanted to protect her from me."

How could I possibly ever be thankful enough to Cousin Will Ann for that? Maybe by somehow seeing that Hank got what he deserved?

"Will Ann paged you at the chamber meeting," I said. "She wanted you to come outside. You answered the page, realized you were in trouble, made suggestions that got the other members out of the way, and went to meet her. Right?"

"Very good, Kitty. Will Ann threatened me with jail right then and there. I mean, really, can you see me in jail?"

Frankly I couldn't, but if there was any way to get out of this,

I was going to. And Hank Lloyd was going to spend the rest of his life in the security prison at Marion, Illinois, the same prison where Pete Rose did his time.

We walked through the kitchen and Hank steered me toward the door that led to the garage. Like the fool I was, I'd straightened up the entire kitchen last night, so there wasn't a single thing lying out on any of the counters that I could use for a weapon, not even a dish towel. I glanced around for Scheherazade, hoping she'd twist around Hank's ankles and distract him, maybe giving me a chance to grab for a weapon. She wasn't in the kitchen, which meant she was probably napping somewhere after her snack.

Now, if we'd been at Maggie's I could probably have picked up a Howitzer among her bowls of apples and oranges, and blown Cousin Hank to Kingdom Come. Which he certainly deserved. Or Tori and Billy could've tackled him. No way he would have gotten away from them.

I felt my eyes tearing up. Would I ever see my lovely grandbabies again? And when Sunny found out what Hank was really like, and that her "friendship" with him had led to Cousin Will Ann's murder, not to mention the death of her own parents, what then?

Best not to think of that now.

I stepped into the garage, Hank close behind me, and called for Jack. Between the country music on the radio and the air compressor running, it took three tries to get his attention. When he turned around and saw Hank with a gun pointed at my side, his face turned so pale I thought he'd pass out. He wiped his face with a rag he'd made out of one of my old sweatshirts.

"Morning, Jack," Hank said. "I'd like to talk to you and Cousin Kitty outside."

Jack didn't move until Hank jammed the gun even harder

into my side. I nearly jumped out of my shoes, and this pair was tied on with double knots.

"Let's go out back and have a chat by the pole barn." Hank pointed to the back garage door, and Jack moved in that direction, glancing at me as if trying to communicate. We'd always been able to read each other's minds, but given that mine was as frozen as home-made ice cream at the moment, I couldn't seem to send or receive messages. I had to do something, but what?

We walked across the rock patio. Hank had "generously" allowed me to take Jack's arm, since I couldn't navigate without some type of support. Which reminded me . . .

"Hank, why did you run me off the road? It was you, wasn't it?"

"Yes, Cousin Kitty, it was me." He heaved a sigh that almost sounded real. "I'm very sorry about that. I meant for you to die right away, not linger for a whole night and day, and certainly not have to work so hard to recover."

How kind. Jack's jaw was working furiously.

"But why?" Dumb question, but I had to ask.

"I saw you sitting at Will Ann's desk the day Patricia Ann asked you over to help sort through her mother's things. You kept your back to me the whole time I was offering you tea. That isn't like you. Your mother raised you to be a polite lady. I knew you had to be hiding something."

Thanks again, Mother.

"After you and Patricia Ann left for home and Craig left to study with Sunny, I fiddled around with the desk until I found that little secret panel."

Jack gave me a look, but I just shrugged. Did Cousin Will Ann's desk have a secret panel? Mine had one, and her desk was like mine, except much more expensive, of course. What had I found in there that made me keep my back to Hank that day?

"I found the file she'd been keeping on me, and the name of the investigator she'd had following me," Hank said, answering my unspoken question. "There was nothing in there about Sunny and me, but I figured you'd go see the P.I. and start digging. Which, of course, you did."

We'd reached the pole barn and Hank ordered us inside. Along with the Chevy and all his antique car paraphernalia, Jack stored his old mower out there. Old mowers could be very deadly if handled incorrectly. I had a feeling I knew how Hank was planning to use it on us.

"I had to get rid of you, Cousin Kitty, so I swiped Maggie's van."

"Everyone knows she leaves her keys in it," I said. "You figured I wouldn't be afraid if I saw a vehicle like hers in my rearview mirror. Then all you had to do was follow me to a safe place. When I headed over that bridge, you guessed where I was going."

Jack's hand tightened on mine, as a warning or in comfort. Then he pulled out his keys and unlocked the pole barn door.

"How did you get Will Ann inside our pole barn that night?" Jack asked. "And why?"

"Simple," I said, wondering why I hadn't thought of it before. "Hank owns a car lot. He must have learned how to open stubborn locks a long time ago, and the one on our old barn is easy. I bet he has master keys at the lot that fit most cars and their trunks."

Hank smiled and with the hand that didn't hold the gun, he gave me a thumb's up. Then, almost boastfully, he pulled a rather large set of keys out of his pocket and jingled them. "I put Will Ann's body into your trunk to throw suspicion on you two, of course. Will Ann said she'd been to Farley's to see you, and that she was on her way to find Sunny. When she turned to leave, I caught her by the neck and strangled her. I didn't plan it, but it worked out just as well. Your jumper cables came in quite handy as a decoy weapon. I think you've probably figured out the rest, Kitty."

I nodded without thinking. Hank pushed open the huge door and led us to the tractor.

"Get on the tractor, both of you," he ordered.

Jack climbed into the seat, then helped me up to stand on the frame beside him.

Hank climbed up on the other side of the frame. "Looks to me like Craig hasn't been mowing quite close enough to the pond," he said. "Weeds like that will draw snakes. Let's see if we can fix it."

A chill slid up and down my back. So that was how he planned to kill us. Overturn the tractor at the pond, most likely on top of Jack. A lot of farmers had died that way. And for me?

Hank looked across Jack at me. "Your girls will think you came out to rescue Jack and you drowned. Don't worry, Cousin Kitty. I'll make sure it's quick this time."

Jack looked grim. I could see he was getting angry, but I didn't want him to do anything foolish with that little gun pointed straight at his lungs. A small firearm that close to his body could do a lot of damage, and Jack Bloodworth was no longer a healthy young football player. I pinched his shoulder.

Jack turned on the engine. It coughed and spluttered, but didn't catch.

"C'mon now, Cousin Jack," Hank said. "I may be a city boy, but I do know enough about tractors to know you have to choke it to get it started." He jabbed Jack's side again with the pistol. "Stop stalling and get this tractor moving."

Jack pulled on the choke, turned the key, and this time the tractor fired up. I wished I could choke Hank. Jack backed the tractor out of the barn and I held on for dear life.

"Why did you steal my purse?" I asked as Jack turned around and headed toward the pond. Might as well keep him talking while there was still time to distract him.

"Because you keep your whole life in there. Will Ann used to laugh about it. I thought you'd never leave it where I could get to it."

He was right. I normally kept it near me wherever I went. I'd only left it in Debby's car that day because it made pushing the walker more difficult. I wondered what he'd have done if I hadn't left it in her car.

Hank, Jack and I had a fairly wild ride to the pond, bumping through the edge of the corn field, jouncing over the stubs left behind where the field had been recently harvested. I tried to glance around to see if maybe John Holmes was nearby. But it was his day to help out at the Senior Center. He wouldn't be home until well after supper. We were on our own.

Or so I thought. As we reached the edge of the pond I heard a cry and looked back. Maggie was running toward us, yelling and waving. "Hey, Mom, Dad, where are you guys going?"

Please, God, no! She had small children to raise, and Hank would have to kill her as well. Most likely the kids were sitting in the van, waiting for their mother to return. Would Hank kill them too?

The tractor lurched as Jack yanked at the wheel. Hank had raised the gun away from Jack's side to point it at Maggie and was caught completely off guard. Jack quickly shifted gears and the tractor spun on one back tire. Jack's arm caught me across the neck and knocked me plumb off the tractor. As I hit the ground, I saw the tractor tip and roll over onto Hank and Jack as it slid downward into the pond.

Chapter Forty-Two

"I have never been so shocked in all my life," Maggie said for the umpteenth time that week. "Cousin Hank a murderer."

I elbowed her into silence and nodded toward her sister, sitting silently on the sun porch stroking the kittens and watching as Craig and Joe unloaded Jack's new tractor off John Holmes's borrowed trailer. Maggie sounded like a broken record. I'd have thought she'd have turned it off by now. She glanced at Sunny's stiff back and bit her lip. Finally, my nudge seemed to have gotten through to her.

Sunny had taken the news about Hank with quiet dignity, but I was sad to note that when she and Craig brought the new tractor over, the young, innocent look had completely died out in her eyes. She'd matured far beyond her years practically overnight, and I prayed someday she'd forgive herself for her relationship with Hank and the disaster it had brought on all of us, particularly Cousin Will Ann.

And that she'd be able to forgive Hank—even though he didn't deserve it—because not forgiving meant it would continue to eat at her. But wanting to forgive and having to forgive because it was the right thing to do were two very different things, as I was quickly learning.

Funny, but I actually missed Cousin Will Ann and our verbal sparring matches. She'd been as prickly as a porcupine, and just about as much fun to try to pet, but her last thought had been to save Sunny from Hank. I'd always be thankful to her for that.

Sunny and Craig's first thoughts had been to save each other, hence the fake alibis that very nearly resulted in Craig's arrest.

I said, "Are you ready to go, Maggie? We're due at the Citizen's Police Academy in thirty minutes and I don't want to be late."

"Not to worry. With me driving, we'll be there in plenty of time."

I was about to protest when Jack said, "Young lady, you'll drive carefully and slowly. Your mother and I have had enough injuries to last us the rest of our lives."

Amen to that. When Jack knocked me off the tractor to save me—or so he'd sworn at the hospital later—I'd broken my leg again, in the exact same place as in the car wreck. Back to crutches for me for the next six weeks, I thought with a sigh. This time I'd be wearing one of those hard plastic braces to keep the leg immobile. At least I could take it off long enough to scratch an itch.

Jack's arm was broken where the tractor tire ran over it. We were a sorry looking pair in our matching braces, but we were lucky to be alive, so no complaining. Well, none on our part.

Both of Hank's legs were broken and his back seriously injured. Jack's old tractor had rolled over on him, and, according to Parker, he hadn't stopped whining since.

I don't think I'll ever forget the last time I saw Hank Lloyd, lying in the shallow part of our pond and spitting up blue mud.

He was now in the psychiatric ward in a Paducah hospital. Not because he was crazy—though, come to think of it, he just might be. The psych ward was, in fact, the most secure area where he could recover without the slightest chance of an escape. Until he could be transferred back to the Massac County Detention Center in downtown Metropolis to await trial for Cousin Will Ann's murder.

And, of course, the attempted murders of Kitty and Jack

Bloodworth.

Parker had recommended that Hank be tried in the state of Illinois, once it was discovered that most of his crimes had actually taken place here.

Maggie said, "Ready, Mom?"

"In a minute." I hobbled to the kitchen door. "Sunny, are you sure you don't want to come with us?"

"Not tonight, Mom. Maybe next time." She kept her gaze fixed firmly on Craig, and I wondered if she was crying and didn't want me to see. I crutched over and gave her a hug.

" 'This too shall pass,' " I quoted, not remembering for the moment where I'd read it. She nodded and squeezed my hand.

Maggie held the back door open and followed me out to her van, where she carefully tucked me into the front seat. Jack looked longingly over his shoulder to where Craig was now steering the new tractor into the pole barn. Joe had walked to the pond, where he was receiving rock-skipping lessons from his children.

I knew Jack was missing the old tractor that he'd so lovingly cared for throughout the years, but the girls had demanded he get rid of it for one that wouldn't tip over as easily as his old one had. Never mind that said tipping over had saved all our lives. I was willing to bet Jack had stashed his old tractor in John Holmes's barn so that he could eventually repair the damage the tip-over into the pond had caused.

Jack sighed and struggled into the back seat. I hoped he wasn't sitting on a bed of animal crackers. The children weren't allowed to attend this evening's event, so it was just the three of us headed over to Paducah to the Citizen's Police Academy, hosted by the Paducah Police Department. As we crossed the bridge, I looked at the sunset, admiring its beauty and thankful I was here to enjoy it.

Parker had politely suggested our family join the Paducah

Citizen's Police Academy after Hank had been safely ensconced in the hospital and my leg and Jack's arm had been set. "You'll be able to see that we actually do know how to do our jobs," he'd said. "And if you insist on helping us solve future crimes, at least you'll have some knowledge of the proper procedures."

I'd always wanted to take the Citizen's Police Academy classes, but even though Metropolis, Illinois is only a few miles from Paducah, Kentucky, there's that pesky river between which puts us into different states. The academy was set up mostly for the Paducah/McCracken County residents to take advantage of, and the waiting list was long. When Parker heard I was dying to participate, he'd gone out of his way to get us in. Tonight was our first class.

Thankfully, when the receptionist buzzed us in through two secure doors, she led us to an elevator. I don't think I could have made it up those marble stairs.

We entered a large room with desks and chairs, populated by several individuals wearing royal blue shirts with CPA on the pockets, just like ours. Maggie was the youngest person in the room. Apparently, most of the class was made up of the older generation, here to learn about the police department and lend support whenever we could.

I scanned the pictures on the wall behind the snack table. Hanging there were shots of the Paducah Police Department from its beginning to the present day. I leaned in closer to stare at a picture dating possibly as far back as the thirties. It depicted an officer standing on the running board of a gorgeous, seemingly new squad car, and I wondered where that car was now. It would be worth a fortune restored to its original glory. And what a hoot it would be for Jack and me to attend car club meetings in something like that.

Jack handed me a cup of coffee, interrupting my daydream and reminding me to find a seat.

On the way to my seat, an officer pressed an informational flyer into my hand about the alumni academy to the CPA, which sounded like a great organization if only I could keep from breaking a leg long enough to participate. The alumni members helped the police department by attending large gatherings in the Paducah area, like the Summer Festival, and reporting problems to the department via walkie-talkies, if they spotted anything suspicious. And alumni members got to participate in some sort of drug-busting practice held for local officers. With one solved murder under my belt, I knew this would be the organization for me.

I couldn't wait for my leg to heal so I could do the ride-along with an officer in a cruiser. Thieves, drug dealers, forgers, bring 'em on. Jack and I could handle them.

The lights went low, the screen lit up at the front of the class room, and I assumed we were ready to begin. Instead, a picture of my poor little crushed Beetle came up on the screen.

Parker stood at the podium. "Folks," he said, "before we begin our first class for this session of the Citizen's Police Academy, I'd like to honor a couple of our participants."

He turned to me. "A would-be killer did this to Kitty Bloodworth's Volkswagen by running her off the road and leaving her to die. She survived in this—" he pointed to the screen "—for over twenty-four hours, with just a small bottle of water and half a granola bar. But she did survive, and she and her husband Jack managed to toss the killer into their pond when he came after her again. Both risked their lives and both were injured bringing him to justice."

Parker approached the desk Jack and I shared. Maggie was sitting on the other side of me, grinning like a possum at lunch. She'd known about this and kept it quiet, the little sneak.

"Mr. and Mrs. Bloodworth, I'd like to present you with this

small gift in honor of your courage in capturing this killer," Parker said.

He handed me the most beautiful plaque I'd ever seen, with our names engraved on it, and I cried. Jack shook Parker's hand and told him not to be a stranger because we nearly always had cake and coffee.

Silly me, I nodded.

"And I trust that you will confine your detecting efforts in the future to this class," Parker said. "We certainly don't want you two chasing down any more killers on your own."

Jack nodded and I gave him a little kick with my good leg. Of course we wouldn't have to chase down any more killers. The only bad apple in our family was currently languishing in a nearby hospital. We couldn't possibly be connected with two such killers in one lifetime.

Could we?

ABOUT THE AUTHOR

Born and raised in Las Vegas, Nevada, **Lonnie Cruse** now resides with her husband in Metropolis, Illinois, home of Superman. She writes the Metropolis Mystery series as well as the Kitty Bloodworth, '57 series. Lonnie is a member of Sisters In Crime, past president of the Internet Chapter, current vice-president of the Mid-TN chapter, Guppys, Heartland Writers Guild, Southern Illinois Writers Guild, and the National Women's Book Association. She and her husband joined the Antique Automobile Club of America and the Southern Illinois Region Ohio Valley Chapter after becoming proud owners of a '57 Chevy. The car is still undergoing restoration. Lonnie can be contacted through her Web site: www.lonniecruse.com.